THE FOURTH I

CHAPTER O

Usually on Sunday mornings, when he is free, Neal Shand likes nothing more than a leisurely walk to his local newsagent to buy his Sunday paper and have a coffee in his favourite cafe.

He is forty-one years old, measures six feet two inches, has a very muscular body, short strawberry blond hair, aquamarine eyes, strong jaw line and a fine straight nose. He enjoys cycling, running and swimming. He boxed for the Police sports club five years running, never losing a fight.

He has a daughter called Molly who is away at university in London studying law. They became even closer when Neal's wife Samantha was tragically knocked down by a drunk driver and died of her injures one week later in the local hospital. That happened just over three years ago, but he still misses her so much he often feels that his heart will burst in his chest every time he thinks of her.

Unexpectedly his mobile phone rings and the distinct tune tells him it is the police station.

'DCI Shand.'

'DCI Shand, can you come straight away. You're needed.'

'Okay. On my way.'

'Shit, today is not starting very well,' he thinks.

He hurries to his old but reliable VW Beetle, a car he has been restoring for many years, always attending the bug fests to make sure he gets only original parts, and drives the five miles to the police station. He walks through the main door, straight to the front desk.

'Morning, Sergeant.'

'Morning, Sir.'

'What's so urgent to call me in on the first Sunday I've had off in weeks?'

'We have a body, Sir.'

'Where is it, Sergeant?'

'Down on the beach, Sir. PC Blake is with it and the person who found it. She's quite shaken up by all accounts. She was walking her dog on the beach at seven this morning when she found it.'

'Is DS Walker here yet?'

'On his way, Sir.'

Detective Sergeant Robert Walker is twenty-five years old, single and lives alone. He is a career police officer who plays football for the police team. He is tall, strong with jet-black hair and a hit with the women especially when he plays his favourite songs on his guitar in the police bar on a Saturday night.

They drive down to the beach together. The view is always stunning. The scenery of the Cornish coastline is one of the most striking in England. The wild and rugged cliffs stand firm against the cloudly morning sky. The crashing waves seem to annoy the seagulls that are circling above hollering their distintive call.

'So, DS Walker, your Sunday is ruined as well?'

'It would seem so, Sir.'

The distinctive sound of the VW Beetle stops as he cuts the engine. As they walk down to the beach, DCI Shand can see Doctor Cole, the forensic examiner, looking over the body.

'Good morning, Doctor Cole.'

'Good morning, Mr Shand.'

'So, what do we have Doctor. Did he drown?'

'No, it's much worse than that I'm afraid.'

'Tell me, Doctor.'

'Well, at first glance he was murdered. These injuries were certainly not self-inflicted.'

'Time of death Doctor?'

'I won't know for sure until I do the post mortem, but I would guess between midnight and six a.m.'

DCI Shand leans closer to take a better look at the body.

'Jesus, what on earth happened here, Doctor?'

'It's hard to say but he has a small nylon rope around his neck, stab wounds to his upper body, and severe facial cuts. Take a closer look at this. His tongue has been torn out, not cut but literally torn out.'

'Any identification?'

'Nothing so far. Whoever did this took everything from his body. But that's your job isin`t it Mr Shand.'

'And the witness?'

'She's waiting over there by the rocks, really shaken up. Not a nice thing to find on a morning walk.'

'No, I can imagine.'

Shand walks towards her introduces himself and and asks her name.

'My name is Annabel Christi,' she answers fumbling a wet hankichief with her fingers, 'I'm from Dublin but I live here now.'

Shand sees a slender young woman with shoulder length flame red hair, emerald-green eyes and an attractive cluster of freckles across her nose. She has a distintive southern Irish brogue when she speaks.

'Miss Christi, I am detective Chief Inspector Shand. I need to ask you some questions. Do you feel up to it? or maybe it would be better if we did this down at the Police station?'

'Please, can we go? I can't look at that body anymore,' she says, tugging on her hair.

'I can imagine. But please don't concern yourself. We will have it removed as soon as possable.'

At the police station DCI Shand shows Miss Christie into the interview room with PC Sally Watson. He turns on the tape recorder.

'I am Detective Chief Inspector Shand. Also present is PC Sally Watson. Could you say your name and address for the tape please?'

'My name is Annabel Christi. I live in Cottage Lane, number 21 in Bonnington, Cornwall.' She answers with strain in her voice still shaking from the sight of the dead body she found on the beach.

'Thank you Miss Christi. Today is the 5th of July. The time is 09.30. Now, Miss Christi, I know this will be hard for you but will you tell me exactly what you saw?'

'Well, every morning I walk my dog Sherper along the beach, usually between six and seven. This morning seemed the same as usual, until Sherper started barking very loudly, which he doesn't usually do,' she says biting her lips while looking down at the floor.

She stops talking, wipes her eyes, takes a deep breath and continues:

'Then I saw the body.'

She looks away as if trying to avoid that morning's scene.

'At first, I thought he must be asleep. You know, out drinking all night. But, 'as I got closer, I could see that he was not sleeping.'

She stops again inhailng deeply as if searching for words.

'Go on, please Miss Christi.'

'Well, as I got a little closer I could see the horrible cuts on his face and upper body. It was awful! I just screamed. I didn't know what to do. Eventually I thought, thank God I have my mobile phone with me so I called the Police.' As she was remembering the scene, she started trembling as if she felt very cold.

'Yes, quite,' said DCI Shand thinking back to what should have been a quiet Sunday morning. If only he had left his mobile phone at home, he would be reading his Sunday paper and drinking a Cappuccino now.

5

'So what did you do then, Miss Christi?'

'Nothing really. I waited over by the rocks until the police arrived. Thank God you arrived quickly I couldn't stand being there all on my own much longer.'

'You didn't touch the body, did you?'

'God, no! I couldn't bear to look at it, let alone touch it.'

'Thank you, Miss Christi. Is there anything else you can think of that might help?'

She wished all this hadn't happened. She just wanted to get away and go home.

'I can't think of anything more right now, it was all so awful. I've never seen a dead body before.'

CHAPTER TWO

'Doctor Cole, have you had a look at our man?'

'Yes, and it's not a pretty site. Come with me.'

Mortuaries are always cold eerie places, with a very unique smell about them, the aroma of death.

'What was the cause of death, Doctor?'

'The stab wound to the heart would have finished him off. A large and very sharp knife, not your normal household type you would see in any kitchen.'

'How do you mean, Doctor?'

'Well, judging by the entry wound I would say it's about six to seven inches long, but very thin. Not a knife for everyday use, more one for symbolic use.'

'I'm sorry, Doctor, I don't understand.'

'What I'm saying, Mr Shand, is that he was killed in a ritual way. This was not a random killing. Someone or several people took their time over this, the pain and suffering must have been horrifying.'

'Go on, Doctor. Please continue.'

'The rope around his neck wasn't actually used. As I said, it seems to be symbolic in some way. At first his eyes must have been gouged out slowly to cause maximum pain. They used some sort of blunt instrument.'

'Such as?'

'Judging by the damage around the eyes I would say a spoon.'

'What you mean, something like a tea spoon or dessert spoon?'

' Yes, Mr Shand, that's exactly what I mean. I would say it was a dessert spoon. You can see where they pushed it in and gouged out the eye leaving it resting on his cheek.'

'Surely, he would have cried out in agony, and someone would have heard it?'

'Yes, you would think so, wouldn't you? But looking at the mutilation to his mouth that would not have been possible.'

'How do you mean, Doctor?'

'As far as I can see he had his tongue torn out at the same time. I already told you about this back on the beach. This tells me that more than one person were present when this was happning.'

'Yes you did, Doctor. Please go on.'

'The tools used to do this would have been very basic, not special in any way, most likely a common pair of workmans pliers. But it would take a man of great strength to do this. Plus he would still have been conscious while all this was going on.'

'How do you know that, Doctor?'

'Because his blood test results show an unusually high dose of Provigil.'

'What's that?'

'It's a drug, that is used to keep someone awake, especially under torture. See the puncture marks on his arm? Dr Cole lifts the arm to show Shand the marks. Whoever did this, Mr Shand, wanted him to experience as much pain as possible until the very last minute before death. Now, the final thing, take a look at this.' Dr Cole holds a small object in his fingers.

'It's a small statue of a monkey, isn't it?' Shand turns it over slowly in his hand and sees something written there.

'Yes, I found it pushed into his mouth after I took the tape off.'

'What does the word *Lwazaru* mean?'

'That is for you to find out, Mr Shand, you're the detective.'

CHAPTER THREE

Bonnignton police station is a hive of activitiy since the discovery of the body. DCI Shand has been put in charge of the investigation.

'Okay, Sergeant, what have you found out about our man?'

'His name is, sorry was Mark Bruley, twenty-eight years old, well known to us, here take a look at his list of convictions.'

'Hmm, a busy boy.'

'Yes, Sir. Most of his life he has been in some sort of trouble. His grandmother reported him missing five days ago. Although this had happened many times before, but he always turned up sooner or later.'

'Not this time, Sergeant. Not alive anyway.'

'No, Sir. Whoever did this wanted to make sure he would never commit any more crimes.'

'And Doctor Cole's report?'

'Here, Sir. Makes for some very macabre reading.'

'Who could do such a thing to another human being, albeit not a very nice one?'

'Difficult to imagine, Sir, but they certainly wanted to make him suffer and understand what he did was wrong before he died.'

'Doctor Cole mentioned something about a ritual knife.'

'Yes, Sir. According to his wounds it was long, about six to seven inches. Very slim for a knife. They used it on him several times to maximise pain. At the same time someone was quite literally pulling out his tongue, which implies more than one person were present while this was going on.'

'But the actual cause of death was the knife through the heart, wasn't it?'

'Yes, Sir. But he was still stabbed many times before the one that killed him.'

'That would have taken someone with medical knowledge, making sure the last one was the one that killed him. Moreover, someone with a very sick mind, Sergeant.'

'That too, Sir.'

'Okay, where do we go from here?'

In an unknown location, Abrithil, the worshipful master of the Freohr answers the phone: 'Yes?'

A shadowy voice starts to speak: 'They found the body. DCI Shand is in charge of the investigation.'

'So?'

'We carry on as usual. They can never find out who we are. I will make sure of that. We should not talk too much on the phone.'

'Okay, see you at the next meeting. The line goes dead'

The order of the Freohr, a group of men who take justice into their own hands when they feel the authorities have let down the public, ridding their environment of violent and dangerous people. Their motto is: 'Se onr sverar sitja hvass,' meaning, 'May your swords stay sharp.'

Back at the police station DCI Shand and Sergeant Walker are getting ready to leave.

'All right, Sergeant, let's call it a day, or what's left of our Sunday. See you in the morning.'

Neal Shand spends the rest of the day polishing his treasured VW Beetle trying to make some sense of what he witnesed this morning.

Annabel Christi is feeling better and less nervous, she therefore decides to go out for a walk to try and clear her head.

'Come on Sherper, let's go. What's wrong with you?'

The dog seems reluctant to go for a walk this evening he looks very sad. Annabel looks down at him, he looks back up with a sulking eyes, droopy ears and an expression of apprehension. He is sitting by the door but distinctively shows he does not really want to go out for a walk.

'Don't worry, we'll go somewhere different tonight.'

Annabel stays up on the cliff top to avoid the beach, which is still taped off as a crime scene. She cannot stop thinking about the horrors she witnessed this morning. Her mobile phone rings shaking her from her thoughts.

'Miss Christi?'

'Yes.'

An unknown voice says: 'If you know what's good for you. You will not say anymore to the police about what you saw this morning on the beach.'

'Who is this?' she asks with a shaky voice but the phone goes dead. She looks at the screen but the number is withheld.

'Shit.'

With shaky fingers she dials another number immediately.

'DCI Shand.'

'Hello, it's Annabel Christi.'

'Hello Miss Christi. How can I help?'

She can hardly speak: 'I've just received a phone call on my mobile.'

'Who from?'

'He didn't give a name.'

'What did he say?'

She tries to remember: 'He said 'If you know what is good for you, you won't say anymore about what you saw on the beach this morning.'

'Anything else?'

'No, he rang off before I could say anything.'

'You said 'He' are you sure?'

'Yes. I'm sure it was a mans voice.'

'Have you heard this voice before?'

'No, sorry. I didn't recognise it.'

'Did you check the number?'

'Yes, but it was withheld.'

'Where are you now?'

'I'm walking my dog, but I'll be home in five minutes,'

'Can I come to see you?'

'Well, I'm a bit worried. What if someone's watching me?' I've just been threatened.

'Good point. But I have to see you, this is serious. Please do not use your mobile anymore until we meet.'

'Okay. Where then?' She would prefer to go home but does not say it.

'There's a tearoom in town called the Willows, it's in Milton road.'

'I know it.'

'Ten minutes then?'

'Okay, see you there.' She immediately heads off to the tearoom.

'What the fuck did you do that for?' came a scream down the phoneline.

'I just wanted to make sure she doesn't say anymore to the police.'

'You fucking idiot! She's probably talking to them as we speak.'

'Sorry. I just thought…'

'Too late for sorry, and don't think. Go and watch her. See where she goes and who she speaks to.'

'Okay. I'm across the road from her cottage now.'

' I'll have to tell the others about this. Don't make any more contact with her, just watch her, and no more fucking phone calls?'

As Annabel enters the cosy tearoom with its distinctive aroma of freshly baked bread. Shand is waiting at a table by the window.

He stands up holding out his hand in a gesture of welcome 'Hello, Miss Christi, how are you?'

'Hello. Please call me Annabel.' She feels confident in Shand's company.

'Thank you, I will. Please take a seat, can I have your phone? There is always a chance we can retrieve the number that called you. I only need it for a day at most. I will get it back to you as soon as I can. I promise.'

'Alright, then.'

As she hands him the phone their fingertips touch. Annabel feels a little flow of electricity pass between them and blushes.

'Are you alright?'

'Yes, I'm fine thanks. Just a bit nervous.'

What is the mater with me? I should be worried about all the events happening to me instead of feeling something for this policeman, she contemplates to herself.

'Okay, I have to go now. I'll call you when I've got some news.'

As they leave the tearoom, they walk off in different directions. A man folding the local gazette under his arm starts to follow Annabel Christi down the street.

Monday morning at the police station, DCI Shand goes to find Sergeant Walker.

'Sergeant, tell me what you've got on Miss Christi's mobile?'

'We have a number, Sir.'

'Good work, Sergeant. Tell me, you have a name as well?'

'I'm afraid not. It's very hard to trace prepaid numbers. You can buy these things anywhere nowadays, even in the local supermarket.'

'I know Sergeant but keep trying. We really need this information.'

'Yes, Sir. I'll get the lab to do their best. I'll take it there now'

Shand is sitting at his desk sorting through his mail. He looks up at Sergeant Walker as he returns to the office.

'We need to talk to the deceased grandmother,' Shand says.

As DCI Shand and Sergeant Walker make their way up the path to Mark Bruley's house, they can't help feeling a little sorry for Mrs Bruley. Her grandson was a criminal but he was all she had for companionship.

They ring the doorbell.

'Mrs Bruley, I am very sorry for the loss of your grandson, but we need to talk to you. Can we come in?'

She hesitates at first but then says: 'Okay. I suppose it's all right.'

'Thank you.'

They enter the house, then she asks them: 'Would you like some tea?'

'No thanks. Maybe later.'

'Tell us, what sort of people did your grandson spend time with?'

'Not very nice ones. I was always telling him they were a bad lot,' tears come to her eyes. She searches for a tissue in her apron.

'Really, in what way?'

'You know, drinking, taking drugs, smoking, and girls, a different one every night. Don't know where he found them. I know he was in trouble with you a lot over the years, but he was the only family I had, since his parents died.' She stops to think: 'That's when Mark turned bad.'

'When was the last time you spoke to him?'

'It would have been last Wednesday, I think. He said he was meeting some friends.' She shakes her head in disgust.

'Do you know any of their names?'

'I know one is called Tony. I don't know about the others, and I don't want to either.'

'Tony what?'

'I'm sorry, I don't remember.'

'Can you describe him?'

'He is quite tall about six feet I would say. I do remember he has a lot of tattoos on his arms, and one on his neck, a spider's web.'

'Are you sure?'

'Yes, I'm sure. He has been here a few times. Nasty person with a foul mouth, always swearing.'

Shand and Walker look at each other both thinking: 'Yes, we know him very well.'

'So, you reported him missing?'

'Yes, when I saw his bed had not been slept in, I got worried and called you lot.

'Thank you, Mrs Bruley, you have been very helpful. We will be in touch when we have something more to tell you.'

'I hope you find the people who did this to him.' They must pay for what they did to my grandson, she shouts at Shand, and Walker.

Shand and Walker leave the house and walk back to their car.

'Okay, Sergeant, let's have a word with our man. We both know who he is, don't we?'

'Yes, Sir. Tony Holland. There is only one like him in town.'

It doesn't take them long to find him. He's always hanging around in the same places. They find him in the local park smoking and drinking a large can of strong beer.

'What do you fucking pigs want?'

'Hello, Mr Holland. Always nice to talk to you.'

'Mark Bruley, you know him, yes?'

'Yeah. So? Pissed again I suppose it's not a crime is it?.'

'No, not pissed, Mr Holland. Dead.'

'What? How?' He seems shocked at the news.

'The how is not important for now. When did you last see him?'

17

'Erm… Last Wednesday. We had a few beers, chatted up a couple of girls, hoping to get lucky, you know what I mean? He winks at Shand and Walker.'

'What time was that?'

'About six, I think.'

'Where did you have these beers?'

'We got a few cans from the local shop, and came here. All the pubs in town have barred us, fucking wankers.'

'And what time did he leave?'

'About eight o'clock, I think.'

'Are you sure? It's very important.'

'Yes, I'm sure it was eight. I went home to watch the football. Useless fucking team lost again.'

'Where did Mark Bruley go?'

'I don't know, all he said was he had to meet with someone about a bit of business.'

'What business?'

'Fucked, if I know. It's none of my concern, and I didn't ask.'

'And that was the last time you saw him?'

'Guess so.'

'Thank you, Mr Holland. You've been very helpful.'

'Whatever, can I go now?'

'Sure, on your way then, bye for now.'

CHAPTER FOUR

As Annabel Christi closes her gate, she looks round anxiously she feels she is being watched, except the street is empty. She enters her cottage just as the home phone starts ringing.

'Hello?'

'Miss Christi, it's DCI Shand.'

'Oh, hello,' she says with relief in her voice.

'Are you alright?' he senses an frightened tone in her voice.

'It's nothing, just me being a bit jumpy.'

'I have your mobile, can I come round to your cottage to return it?'

'Yes, I suppose it's okay.'

'Okay, I'll be there in ten minutes.'

When Neal Shand walks up the path to Annabel Christi's cottage he thinks to himself: 'This Miss Christi is an eye-catching woman.' He rings at the door and waits.

'Hello, Mr Shand.'

'Hello Annabel, how are you?'

'I'm okay, I guess, still a bit shaken up with all this business of that poor boy.'

'Yes, I can imagine, we retrieved a number.'

'That's good, isn't it?' sounding relieved.

'I hope so, but it's very difficult to trace names to prepaid numbers. However, we will keep trying:'

'So, you're no closer then?' her voice seems disappointed.

'We are making some progress, but these things take time. Are you sure you're all right? You seem to be a little preoccupied.'

'Well, it's just that as I got home earlier I had the feeling someone was following me but I didn't see anyone. Just my imagination running wild after what I saw yesterday morning on the beach I suppose. Anyway, would you like a drink, Mr, Shand?'

'Yes, that would be nice but on one condition.'

'What's that Mr Shand?'

'That you please call me Neal.'

The phone conversation is getting heated between the two Freohr.

'So where did she go?'

'The local tearoom, Milton Road called the Willows.'

'Did she speak to anyone?'

'Yes, that policeman. What's his name.'

'Shand?'

'Yes, that's the one. They sat at the same table. She gave him her mobile phone. They talked for another five minutes or so, and then went their different ways. I followed her back to her cottage.'

'If they trace that phone number to you, I'll fucking kill you myself?'

'Don't worry, it's prepaid. I bought it from an old friend who didn't want it anymore. It's untraceable.'

'I hope so for your sake. Now go back and watch her .We may have to have another word with Miss Christi but for now we have more important matters to deal with. We have a new candidate, so be there this evening.'

'Brother Vardens, tonight we have another criminal that walked freely on our streets.'

    The old Castle is the perfect place for their meetings, far away from any houses and roads. The local council had it cordoned off because of structural damage, and no one would ever find out that it is being used for such savage acts.

    Bonnington Castle on the Cornish peninsula was built in the 13th century from stone and rubble. It is situated between Boscastle and Treknow, and Port Isaac bay. The castle has over one hundred steep steps and the nearest parking is six hundred meters away. It is joined to the mainland by a narrow neck of land and faces toward the Atlantic sea. Two tunnels run beneath the island, the shorter one opening up to a meadow above. The longer one taking people to the beach is known as Merlin's Cave. Stout walls and rugged windswept cliff edges encircle a great ruined hall.

Five men are standing in a circle, each one garbed in blood red ceremonial robes, with a silver dagger hanging in a leather scabbard tied around their waist. For the work they are about to perform they need discreet lighting. They do not bother to cover their faces; the 'candidate' will not be leaving with them.

    'Brother Varden, whom have you here?'

The candidate, who they kidnapped earlier the same day, is already in the stone walled hall, shuddering with fear, standing totally naked with a strong fisherman's line secured around his neck, his numb hands tied firmly behind his back. The vile odour of his sweat fills the room. A grimy rag soaked in sour vinegar has been pushed into his mouth and secured with tape. He can scarcely breathe, his nostrils flaring fast and furious with terror. Even though it is bitterly cold in the hall he is sweating and shaking uncontrollably.

A harsh voice speaks out:

'You have committed the crime of rape for which you were never punished. For two years you have walked freely on our streets, flaunting our laws. But no more! Bring the candidate closer.'

The force of the blow to his back with a large wooden club is so violent it knocks him to his knees and makes him urinate all over his body. Two of the Brethren grab an arm each and drag him to the centre of the circle of men, dropping him on his face; the rough stone floor causing a deep cut to his cheek. The Brethren then move back to their places surrounding the chilling scene.

The voice calls out again:

'Brother Varden, are you ready?'

'I am, Master Ebrithil.'

'Turn him over.'

Two other Brethren move from the circle, and start kicking him in his chest, then in his face and finally all over his body so brutally that he feels like vomiting. He curls up with pain. He feels like crying out. They then grab him and as they turn him on his back, they see he has an erection.

'Wait!'

Brother Ebrithil walks from his place, looking down at the victim pointing at his penis, a contemptuous smile appearing on his face.

'You have raped innocent girls, and women with that but you won't need it anymore, not where you're going.'

He speaks to one of the Brothers:

'Varden, you know what to do.'

The sound of the silver dagger being drawn from its scabbard fills the victim with deadly fear. The horrifying and excruciating pain as the blade slices through his penis is so powerful he can hear himself scream but the soaked rag taped to his mouth stops him from being heard. The Brother takes his time enjoying cutting slowly to take full advantage of his macabre task. The victim twists with excruciating pain, blood flowing over his legs. He tries to open his damp crimson eyes but all he can see through a cloud of tears is a Brother standing with his penis in his hands holding it up like a trophy.

Finally the Brother drops it on his tortured body, and walks slowly back to his place, exceptionally satisfied with himself. The victim's sticky blood is pouring from his wound like a fountain onto the cold floor.

'Brother Varden, don't stop yet, please complete your task.'

The Varden strolls back and draws his polished dagger again. At this point, the victim faints. He is covered in urine, blood and vomit which is seeping through the rag in his mouth.

'Varden, we need to wake him up. Give him the injection.'

The dose of Provigil another Varden injects is immediately affective. The victim opens his fuzzy eyes but all he can see is someone standing over him with his dagger drawn.

'Are you ready, my friend?' he says grinning at him.

The first ear is cut off with ease, blood spurting out, the second one is cut off slowly as if the Varden were slicing a loaf of bread, unhurriedly moving backwards and forwards, the warm blood dripping on his hands. By now the victim is anaesthetized and seems to feel no pain. The Varden then stands, like the other one before him, both ears in his hands showing his work of art to the rest of the gathering.

Suddenly another Brother walks toward the body and starts thrusting into it. It is neither the first nor the second stab that kills the victim, but the third one which goes straight through the heart, blood gushing out into the sickly smelling air.

'It is done.'

The blood, urine and vomit will eventually drain away; no one will ever be able to tell what happened here tonight.

The local police patrol is parked near the castle. PC Blake and PC Argent are having a cigarette.

Suddenly PC Blake says: 'What's that?'

PC Argent replies: 'I don't see anything.'

'I thought I saw a flicker of light coming from the old castle?'

'Must be a trick of the light coming off the sea. It's been abandoned for years now; no one ever goes there anymore.'

'I guess you're right want another cigarette?'

'Why not, looking at his watch. 'I think it is going to be a long and boring night.'

CHAPTER FIVE

Arthur Ambrose, the local butcher, is average height and build, and not a sort of person you would notice on the street. He likes a pint of beer at the pub most nights after he closes his shop. He plays bowls on Sunday mornings for the town team. He has been married to Jennifer for 30 years. They have three sons and one daughter who all have left home some time ago. He has worked hard to keep the business running, making his shop one of the finest butchers in town. It is always immaculate with meat and other goods in the window display. His trustful clientele are mostly locals although his reputation brings others from further a field. A woman enters his shop.

'Morning, Mrs Young. What can I do for you today? A nice piece of rump steak, maybe?'

'Yes, that sounds lovely, why not.'

He cuts the meat with extreme care weighs it and hands it over to his client.

'There you are, anything else?'

'No, I think that's all for today, thank you.'

'Shall I add it to your monthly bill?'

'Yes, please.' She waits for him to write it down

He gets out a notebook and adds the amount to her bill.

'Good bye, Mrs Young. I hope to see you again soon,' he says.

'Yes, good bye Mr Ambrose.'

He is pleased with himself as he closes the door of the shop. He cannot stop thinking about last night's event. As he sliced the steak it reminded him of how he hacked off the candidate's penis, and how much he enjoyed it. A little too much maybe, hoping the next one will be just as gratifying. He mutters to himself:

'I must take longer next time, make these bastards suffer more.'

The upstairs room in the Celtic Knot pub, which is usually reserved for the local cricket team meetings, is the perfect place for the Freohr to meet and discuss recent events.

'It was a very successful ritual, I'm very proud of you all. Another appalling and disgusting man who will no longer commit any crimes has been taken care of. Did you dispose of the body as I instructed?'

'Yes, Worshipful Master, he will be found soon. The police will be kept busy, we are safe. No one will ever be able to connect us to the body, or what remains of it.'

'You left no trace at the Castle?'

'No, no one will ever be able to tell what happened there. The recent heavy rains helped to wash away the blood, urine and vomit from the hall'

'Do we have a new candidate?'

'Yes, we have chosen another one, but we must wait.'

'Why?'

'He has been in the local newspaper recently, and it's too soon after the last ceremony.'

'When then?'

'At least two weeks. But we are watching him, don't worry, he will be ours soon enough.'

'Okay, anything else?'

The four others gesture their heads to signal the meeting is finished.

'All right then, go about your business as usual, we will meet again soon.'

The bar down stairs is very busy for a Friday night. Nobody notices them leaving. Harvey Ventura, the landlord of the Celtic Knot walks slowly back behind the bar, and talks to his customers as he would on any normal night.

Annabel decides to go for a long walk with Sherper. She is feeling a little better now, starting to cope with the events although the horror of that day on the beach will never leave her.

It is a beautiful warm sunny day, just right for a walk. She will try hard to forget the past events and think about nothing. Although the Cornish countryside is as picturesque as its coastline she still cannot bring herself to walk down by the beach. Deeply in thought she does not notice the sky blue VW Beetle passing her by.

Neal Shand had a similar idea on this sunny warm day. Only his one is to drive in his beloved car, returning from another bug fest with several items for his vehicle, which he doesn't really need. He suddenly sees Annabel Christi walking her dog and pulls up beside her, slowly not to frighten her.

'Hello, Miss Christi. Enjoying your walk?'

'Yes, thanks. What a lovely car.'

'Thank you. I have put a lot of time and money into it. I hope it's all worth it.'

As he talks, she thinks to herself: 'he is a handsome man, I wonder if he would take me up on an offer of dinner?'

'Mr Shand, sorry, I mean Neal. I was wondering if you are free, that is?'

'Yes?'

She hesitates: 'Well, say 'no' if you want to but would you like to come to my cottage for dinner one night?' Oh dear, she thinks to herself, what if he says no. I'll look really stupid.

Shand is surprised by the invitation but is quite willing to accept.

'I would love to, when were you thinking of?'

'Is tonight too soon?' Why am I in such a hurry to invite this man she agonizes with herself?

'No, not at all. What time?'

'About seven thirty for eight?'

'Perfect, I will see you later then. Thank you.'

He was about to drive off when he turns back to her:

'What will you cook so I can bring the right wine?'

'My speciality is Paella. I hope you like it?'

'I'm sure I will. See you later, and thank you once again.'

Shand is feeling good. It is a lovely day and it will finish pleasantly too.

Annabel runs the rest of the way home thinking: 'God, I have nothing in the
fridge. I'd better go shopping, and fast.'

As she anxiously waits for her guest, Annabel checks and re-checks the table, the hob in the kitchen and the meal she has spent all afternoon preparing. She keeps looking at her watch, thinking: 'Why does time go so slowly when you're waiting for someone.' At last, the distinct sound of the Beetle pulling up outside the cottage tells her he has arrived. Her heart starts beating faster. She looks at herself in the mirror one last time saying to herself: 'I hope he doesn't notice how nervous I am.'

Neal spends a moment in his car thinking to himself: 'This is the first date I have had since Samantha was killed in that tragic car accident but I know she wouldn't mind.' They had talked about it once. If ever one of them were taken prematurely the other one should feel free to move on, and maybe find someone new. Shand grips the steering wheel and looks into the rear view mirror telling himself: 'Just enjoy the evening, she really is a very lovely looking woman and it was, after all, she who asked you.'

As he opens the gate he sees the silhouette of Annabel standing behind the glass of the front door ready to open it. A firm knock brings her back to reality.

'Good evening, Neal. Perfect timing.'

'Good evening, the Paella smells lovely.'

'Oh, it's quite easy. I've made it several times before.

'Really? Tell me what is it that smells so wonderful?'

It's the saffron and the different kinds of fish I use. Plus the rice and herbs I put in it, and of course my own special ingredient, which will remain a secret. An old family tradition. I'm sure you understand?'

'Of course I do. It's a good job I brought the wine with me. A *Cune* rosé. It will complement the food perfectly, I am sure.'

'Yes, I'm sure too. How about an aperitif?'

'Okay, I'm completely in your hands tonight.'

Before she walks to the kitchen, she thinks to herself: 'I wish he hadn't said that all sorts of ideas are running through my brain.'

'Take a seat. I'll be back in a moment.'

'Is there anything I can do to help?'

'No. You are my guest tonight. I hope you'll enjoy yourself?'

'I am sure I will, thank you.'

The evening goes perfectly, the Paella is a success, and the wine is excellent. Both Neal and Annabel feel very relaxed in each other's company, discussing all kinds of topics.

Suddenly, Neal looks at his watch.

'I don't believe it.'

Annabel looks at him wide eyed asking: 'What?'

'It's one in the morning. I had better get going. I have to be at the Police station at eight tomorrow, or should I say today?'

'Okay.' She gets up and sees him to the front door.

'Thank you for a very special evening.'

'You're very welcome Neal. I enjoyed it immensely.'

He thinks to himself: 'Should I kiss her on the cheek or just shake hands.' She makes it easier for him by leaning forward and giving him a peck on his cheek.

'See you soon I hope. Drive carefully.'

For the first time since the death of his wife, Shand feels slightly embarrassed, his face going a little red.

The drive to the police station is merrier this morning. Neal keeps thinking about the previous night.

'Morning, Sergeant Walker.'

'Morning, Sir. You look a little tired, late night?'

Shand looks at his Sergeant, thinking: 'Yes, it was and very enjoyable as well,' but says nothing.

'So what's new, Sergeant?'

'Well, Sir, I'm afraid we have another body.'

'What? Where?'

'In the car park by the cliffs. The local security patrol checked around midnight, because they saw car lights had been left on. They found him in the boot, it wasn't locked.'

'Do we know who he is?'

'Not yet, Sir, that will take some time. He's horribly mutilated.'

'How do you mean?'

'I think we should go and see for ourselves Sir. I have called Doctor Cole. He should be there by now.'

'Okay, Sergeant, lets get there as fast as possible.'

As Shand and Walker approach the parking they see Doctor Cole looking into the boot of a vehicle.

'Good morning, Doctor Cole, can I have a look?'

'If you want, Mr Shand. But I warn you, it's not a pretty site.'

'Jesus, what in God's name happened to him?'

'I won't know for sure until I can get a better look at him back at the morgue.'

'Whoever did this was not worried about hiding it.'

'No, Mr Shand, it would appear not.'

'Seal off the car park, Sergeant.'

32

CHAPTER SIX

'Doctor Cole, give me the details, please?'

'Well, Mr Shand, to start with he was beaten very badly. It looks like some sort of club was used on him. It would have been more than one man doing this at the same time.'

'How can you tell, Doctor?'

'Because the bruising all around his body is equal, that means two or more people were beating him, most likely while he was tied to a post or something similar.'

'Okay, Doctor, go on please.'

'Well, after they finished the beating, they must have stripped him naked and tied his hands with a nylon cord. See the marks on his wrists? Then someone cut off his penis.'

Shand and Walker stare at the Doctor in disbelief: 'What?'

'It's been removed from his body, Mr Shand. Someone cut it off.'

'Why would they do that?'

'Pain, Mr Shand, excruciating and unbearable pain. And look here. See the puncture marks on his arm? They used Provigil again to keep him awake. The same as the last one.'

'And the actual cause of death, Doctor?'

'The same as the first victim, a stab wound straight through the heart but not until they had stabbed him several times all over his body before. But there's more.'

'Go on, Doctor?'

'Before the fatal stab wound they cut off both his ears. And I found this, it's the same as the last one, a small statue of a monkey, but this one has a different inscription.'

'Show me, please, Doctor?'

'It says, *Kikazuru*.'

'Anything else, Doctor?'

'No, Mr Shand, I think that's all. If I discover anymore I will let you know.'

'Okay Sergeant, let's get back to the police station. We have a lot of work to do.'

At the police station Shand and Walker busy themselves researching the meaning to the monkeys.

'These words, Sergeant, have you found any significance to them?'

'Yes, Sir. The first one was *Mizaru*. It's old Japanese from the 17th century and it means, 'See no evil.'

'And the second one?'

' *Kikazaru*, means 'Hear no evil.'

'So we have someone or several people killing in the name of the three wise
monkeys, do we?'

'It's certainly starting to look like it, Sir.'

'Shit, this then tells us one thing, doesn't it?'

'What's that, Sir?'

'It means, Sergeant, there will be another body, a third victim.'

'Tell me, Sergeant, what do we know about this last one?'

'His name was Paul Fletcher, 24 years old, single. He was well known to us.'

'Go on, Sergeant?'

'Rape, attempted rape, child molestation, burglary, theft, and of course a drug addict.'

'It would seem that these people, whoever they are, want to rid us of our criminal fraternity. Some sort of ritualistic gathering of men.'

'Freemasons, Sir?'

'No, Sergeant. Freemasons just keep a very old tradition alive. My Farther was one. I don't believe for one minute they'd do something like this. It's not what they are known for. Freemasons are a nonviolent fraternity. They do good and help all kinds of charities.'

'Who then, Sir?'

'I wish I knew Sergeant. But for now we must try to find out who's behind this. I've asked Doctor Cole to keep it as quiet as he can, for the moment at least. Unfortunately I don't think we have long before it gets into the papers. It's going to be difficult to keep two murders quiet.'

The desk sergeant calls up to Shand's office.

'Sir, your daughter is on the phone.'

'Put her through, please.'

'Hi Dad, it's Molly.'

'Hello, darling, how are you?'

'Okay, a bit tired, I've had exams all this week. I was thinking when I finish, can I come down for a few days?'

'Of course, I would love to see you. It's been too long. When were you thinking of?'

'Well, Saturday morning. I can get the 08.05 and be with you in time for lunch. What do you think?'

'Perfect. I'll meet you at the railway station.'

'Okay. So have you been busy?'

'Oh, you know the usual stuff. A policeman's lot and all that.'

'Very funny. I'll see you Saturday. Bye for now.'

His heart is racing just thinking about Molly. She reminds him so much of his late wife. He misses them both very much. Without Molly, his life would have no meaning.

In the upstairs room at the Celtic Knot, the Freohr gather discussing the events of last week.

'Talk normally, please. We don't know who might be listening.'

'What do the police think?'

'Don't worry, they're as puzzled as we hoped. Shand is young and clever, but it will still take him a long time to work everything out. As long as we behave normally and don't talk outside of this room, we are safe.'

'What about the next candidate?'

'We are still watching him. He has no idea who we are, or what we have in store for him. His time will come.'

A big smile comes across the Freohr's face just thinking about what they will do to the next one.

CHAPTER SEVEN

Annabel Christi is a freelance journalist. She came from Dublin because of a job offer two years ago. These days after that horrible discovery on the beach she tries to concentrate on her work, except reporting local news can be a bit monotonous. The local fair and a new hospital wing do not get the blood flowing. The occasional local television news slot helps, it makes her feel a little glamorous. She still wishes a good story would come her way. However, living in a small Cornish town does not always bring the most exciting news. As she turns the page of her favourite national newspaper, she cannot believe what she sees.

'Jesus Christ, what the hell is going on?' she says to herself. How did the big nationals get hold of this before the local papers. I know one person who can tell me.

Neal Shand is busy with recent events, when the phone rings for at least the hundredth time in the last hour.

'DCI Shand.'

'It's Annabel Christi.'

'Hello, Annabel, always lovely to hear from you. How can I help?'

'I have just read about the murder in the newspaper, can I come to see you to discuss this?'

'Well, as you can imagine I am very busy. I am in charge of the case.'

'When then? It's for my paper. The nationals got the story but we weren't told about it.' She sounds disappointed.

'Yes, I know. Sorry about that. I've been trying to keep it quiet.'

'You owe me an interview.'

'Okay. How about we do this and have dinner at the same time? I have been meaning to call you but it's been so frantic around here.'

'Okay, where and when?'

'My place tonight, about seven?'

'Okay, see you then.'

Annabel feels let down, Neal knows she is a journalist. She is determind to get the story from him.

38

It is Shand's turn to feel nervous as he prepares the table for dinner. As he hears footsteps on his path he moves fast to be ready to open the door. When he does, he
Is struck by a vision of exquisiteness. Annabel is standing there looking stunning. She is wearing a two piece blue outfit with a short skirt, exposing her stunning shapely
suntanned legs. She looks at him waiting to be asked inside but Shand stands rigid to the spot, he can't take his eyes off of her.

'Aren't you going to ask me in or are we going to have dinner on your door step?'

Shand blinks his eyes to bring himself back to reality.

'Yes, of course, I'm sorry. Please come in.'

Over dinner the conversation runs from one topic to another until Annabel asks:

'So, Neal, what is going on in our town? And why did the nationals get the story before I did?'

'Well, the first part will take a long time to tell. As for the nationals getting it first, it had to be, I'm afraid. This thing is getting too big for a local paper to handle.'

'One dead body, that I discovered personally on the beach, remember?'

'Yes, I remember, but I'm afraid it's not one anymore. There are two dead bodies now.'

'What? When? How?'

'Two days ago, we found another one in the boot of a car on the panoramic cliff top parking.'

'Tell me all about it?'

Annabel kicks off her shoes and gets comfortable on Neal's settee, curling her long legs up to a comfortable position. Indicating she is ready to listen. Neil sits opposite in the single chair.

'Much the same as the first, some sort of ritual killing. He was horribly tortured. I can't describe what happened to him, it's too horrifying. In all my years as a police officer I've never seen anything like this. One strange thing though.'

'What?'

'Well, even the nationals don't have this information yet, so keep it to yourself please.'

'I'll try she says taking a sip of wine.'

'We found small wooden statues of monkeys.'

'Go on?'

'The first statue meant, 'See no evil'. The second meant, 'Hear no evil'. You know the story of the three wise monkeys?'

'Yes. I know the story but what does it have to do with these murders?'

'We don't know yet, but it's the only clue we have for now. Sergeant Walker is working on it. I hope he comes up with something, and fast.'

'Me too. You know what this means, don't you?'

'Yes, Annabel. I had already worked that one out for myself. There is going to be a third murder.'

'Do you have any idea as to who could be doing this?'

'Not yet, but sooner or later we will find the people responsible. They can't hide forever.'

Annabel thinks to herself, hopefully sooner.

'Do you think they're local people?'

'Normally, I would have said no but the phone call you got warning you to keep quiet tells me that, yes, they could be people we know, even people we see every day. It's really disturbing to think we might actually know some of them, can you keep this out of the local papers.'

'I don't think so. It's already hit the nationals and my editor is screaming for a front-page story. We can't keep this silent any longer. Besides the local residents need to know what's going on in their own town, don't you think? Maybe they could help, you know, keep an eye out.'

'Neighbourhood watch you mean?'

'Yes, why not?'

'I was hoping to keep it under wraps a little longer. When word gets out, it gets much harder to keep under control. The town will be full of these gory sightseers, you know the kind who love to see blood.'

'I know Neal, but tonight we should shut all this out. How about another glass of wine?' Annabel sits on the sofa with her arm outstretched holding the empty glass smilling a bewitching smile.

CHAPTER EIGHT

Adrian Jarvis is not a nice individual. At twenty-one years old he never held down a job. He relies on unemployment benefit for his money and his mother to give him anything he wants. A slap to her face too remind her that he is now the man of the house since his farther just upped and left one day without a word. He is always in trouble with the police for petty crime, but mostly theft. He rose up the criminal ladder the day he sexually abused the twin Jones sisters of thirteen years old, who were just playing in their local park. Unfortunately they were, and still are, too scared to talk about it, because Jarvis threatens to slit their throats if they ever spoke of what he had done. So he walks free and carries on doing what he likes. The day he walks into the Celtic Knot pub is the worst mistake he ever makes. The landlord spots him straight away drinking at the bar.

'Morning, Mr Jarvis, can I get you another one?'

'You buying?'

'Yes, why not. I always try to make my customers feel welcome.'

'Okay then. I'll have a large whisky, your beer tastes like warm piss.'

As Harvey Ventura pours the whisky, he thinks to himself, enjoy your drink you obnoxious little fuck, it could very well be your last.

He gives Jarvis his drink and walks away to make a phone call.

In the Celtic Knot, Adrian Jarvis is getting very drunk. He can't understand why he keeps getting free drinks, but he thinks to himself, what stupid bastards, if they keep buying, I'll keep drinking.

'Landlord, how about a double this time?'

'Okay, young man, no problem. Anything else?'

'Yeah, I need some fags and a light.'

'My pleasure.'

Harvey Ventura looks at him smiling, telling himself that it is worth it. When we get him to the Castle he will trouble us no longer.

A black van pulls up near the rear of the Celtic Knot. Two men sit and wait. Not a word is said. Harvey Ventura sees the van and signals to it. The two men get out.

'Wait here. I'll bring him to you.'

As he walks back into the bar, he sees Jarvis talking to one of his locals.

'Fuck it, we can't take the risk to snatch him now, people will remember him.'

He returns to the back door, walks out to the car park and talks to the two men standing there.

'Not just yet, my brothers. He's talking to some people in the bar. We'll have to wait. Be patient.'

The two men walk away again, not saying a word.

Neal is cooking his daughter something when she appears downstairs holding a lipstick in her hand.

'Is there something you want to tell me, Dad?'

He looks at her and can feel his face going red.

'Yes, there is one thing I want to talk to you about?'

'Go on. I'm listening?'

He feels like a young schoolboy telling his mother a story.

'Sit down Molly, have something to eat.'

'I can eat and listen at the same time.'

'Okay. Well, I have met someone.' Indeed someone I really like.

'Who, it would appear, wears apricot coloured lipstick?'

'Yes, well it's not mine,' he confesses with a smile

'I should hope not. Go on.' Molly is sitting at the breakfast table lookng very curious.

'Her name is Annabel Christi. She's a journalist for the local Gazette. We met because she was actually a witness to a murder we have had here.'

'Yes I read something in the papers.'

'Well, anyway we have been seeing a lot of each other. We get on really well. Our jobs bring us together sometimes. I would like you to meet her and she wants to meet you too. I've told her all about you. He hesitates, 'so, what do you say?'

'Dad, if you're happy then I'm happy. I would love to meet her.'

Neal is relieved his daughter takes to his new relationship with ease.

Adrian Jarvis is getting very drunk, but he doesn't care anymore. as the drinks are all free, he feels he has won the Lottery.

'Okay, landlord. How about another whisky?'

'No problem, my friend. A large one, is it?'

'I'm going for a piss don't let my whisky get cold.'

Jarvis is laughing loudly, throwing his head back as he staggers down the corridor to the toilet. Harvey Ventura looks at Jenny, his barmaid.

'Look after the bar, would you? I'm going for a lie down for a while, we have a darts' match tonight, so I want to rest for a couple of hours.'

Ventura signals to the two men in the black van waiting in the car park. He joins Jarvis who is standing at the urinal wavering because of all the whisky he drank. He looks at Ventura and slurs:

'I hope you're not looking at my cock, you dirty old man,' he then laughs aloud pushing his head back to accentuate his humour. What he doesn't see are two men standing behind him, one holding a rag, and the other a rope.

Jarvis dosen't feel a thing, the alcohol and morphine knock him out immediately he falls into their arms like a rag doll.

'Don't make any noise, the bar still has a couple of customers in it.'

'Don't worry, we'll be careful with him,' a big grin appearing across their faces.

The black van drives away slowly from the Celtic Knot car park, heading to the Castle. No one takes any notice.

When the van reaches the entrance to the cave Jarvis starts to move, waking up slowly. The rag soaked in morphine makes him want to vomit.

Arthur Ambrose leans over to remove the rag.

'We don't want you dying on us too soon, do we?'

Jarvis looks up and tries to scream, 'what the fuck are you doing?'

'Be patient, young man, soon all will become clear to you.' At that point he pushes another rag into his mouth, this one soaked in morphine.

'He will be out cold for hours. No need to worry.'

'Just make sure he is tied up properly and can't get away.'

The underground caves at the Castle make a perfect jail for their prisoner. No one will hear any screams from down there. The sounds of the waves are a perfect solution to any noise Jarvis could make.

'Don't let the little fucker drown and spoil our fun. The others will be very disappointed if they can't have their way with him.'

The two Freohr stand looking at their prisoner and sneer: 'Don't run away, we will be back later.'

Jarvis can't understand what is happening to him. The mixture of whisky and morphine has a strange effect on him. He keeps coming to and fro from consciousness.

Abrithil is dictating a letter when the phone rings.

'Yes.'

A voice very dark and calm speaks:

'We have him.'

'Okay, do nothing, we will meet later. Usual place and time.'

'Okay.'

The phone goes dead. Abrithil speaks to his secretary:

'Is that it for today, Alice?'

'Yes, we are finished.'

'Okay then. I will take advantage of getting away early. See you tomorrow.'

In the upstairs rooms at the Celtic Knot pub the Freohr meet.

'So tell me. Where is he?'

'Don't worry, he is safe. We have put him in the smugglers cave a long way in. No one will find him.'

'What about the tide?'

'He is high up, enough to keep clear of it.'

'And have you tied him up? We don't want him getting away.'

'He is chained to the rock. He isn't going anywhere.'

'Okay, when then?'

'I think we should wait a day or two. It's still too soon after the last one.'

'Very well. But someone should bring him some food, we don't want him starving to death.'

Neal Shand cannot remember being this nervous before a meeting of his daughter with his new girlfriend. The two most precious people in his life. However he still cannot help feeling guilty when he thinks about his late wife Samantha.

'Wow, Dad, the table looks lovely. What are we having for dinner?'

'My speciality of course.'

'Oh, so that means spaghetti bolognaise, does it?'

'Yes, but wait until you taste my new source.'

'Well, it does smell absolutely wonderful.'

'Okay go and open the wine. Let it breath for a while.'

He checks the table and the food again while he is waiting for Annabel to arrive. Any minute now he tells himself.

The doorbell rings, and Neal's heart almost misses a beat.

'Shall I get the door, Dad?'

'No, let me.'

As he opens the door he sees what can only be described as a vision of magnificence. Annabel is standing there looking so terribly striking he can hardly talk. His mouth drops open.

'Seen enough, lover?'

'Yes, I'm sorry. Please come in. Let me take your coat.'

They walk into the living room where Molly is waiting.

'Dad, you never told me she was a super model.'

Annabel walks straight over to Molly and gives her an embrace.

'It's lovely to meet you at last. Your father talks about you all the time.'

'Thank you, Annabel. It's lovely too meet you too. I cannot believe how gorgeous you look. Your flowing red hair is amazing. Is it natural?'

'Yes, it's all mine. Your father is a very lucky man to have two such beautiful women in his life, don't you think, Neal?'

They both laugh.

'Yes, I do,' admits Neal.

'How about a glass of wine?'

Arthur Ambrose and Frank de Caux make their way to the smuggler's cave.

'Can we have a little fun with him?'

'What do you mean?'

'Just enough, to scare the shit out of the little cunt.'

'We were told to give him food and water, just enough to keep him alive until we're ready. Even so, we should make him aware he is in the middle of the worst fucking shit storm he will ever be in.'

'True. I suppose we can enjoy ourselves a little. It's not as if he can complain about us, can he?' They both laugh aloud.

The crashing of the waves drowns out all noises anyone makes.

'So, young man, are you comfortable?'

'Who the fuck are you? What do you want?'

They lean close to Jarvis.

'We're here to see that you never look at any young girls again. Let alone sexually molest them. Do you understand? You revolting little fuck.'

'I don't know what you're talking about, let me go.'

'Don't be stupid Jarvis. We both know that's not going to happen, don't we?'

They both start kicking him violently in his testicles.

Then they walk away taking no notice of Jarvis' screams.

The evening is going better than Neal had anticipated. Annabel and Molly are getting on exceptionally well. They are talking like two sisters and Neal can hardly get a word in. He just sits there looking and thinking to himself that he is a very lucky man.

Molly looks at her father.

'Okay, Dad, we will do the dishes. You make the coffee.'

'My pleasure.'

'I'm just going to powder my nose, back in a minute,' says Molly.

Annabel puts her arms around Neal's waist and gives him an affectionate hug.

'Neal, she's so lovely and I think we are getting along really well.'

'Yes, I think so too. I could hardly get a word in. But I'm happy. I was very anxious about tonight.'

'So, do you think I can stay here with you this evening?'

'I don't think Molly will have a problem with it. I want you to stay.'

The desk Sergeant at the police station has just made himself a cup of tea when the
phone rings.

'Bonnington Police?'

'Oh, hello. I want to report my son missing.'

'Can I take a few details? How long has he been missing?'

'Well, only a few hours. But he's always home for his dinner. I don't understand why he is not here.'

'Okay. Give me his name, please?'

'Adrian Jarvis.'

'And you're his mother. Is that right?'

'Yes. He is all I have since his father died.'

'The thing is, Mrs Jarvis, there isn't much we can do until he has been missing for twenty four hours. And it's not against the law to miss your dinner. I'm sure he will be home as soon as he gets hungry. I will make a note of it and tell the patrol cars to keep a look out for him. Can I have a description of him?'

As the Sergeant puts the phone down, he thinks to himself, why do I know this name?

In the upstairs room at the Celtic Knot, the Freohr are talking about their next ceremony.

'I think it's still too soon. The police are still very active on the last two deaths. We can't risk it.'

'So what do we do with him?'

'He'll have to stay exactly where he is. We can't let him go now can we? He has seen some of your faces.'

'Okay, go and see he's still there. Make sure he doesn't get away. If he does we all go to jail.'

Sergeant Walker is the first one in the office looking through the reports of the last two murders.

'Morning, Sergeant.'

DCI Shand sits down at his desk.

'Morning, Sir.'

'Tell me what you have so far?'

'Well, Sir, we have a pattern between the two victims. The style of the killing is practically identical. It is without a doubt some kind of ritual killing. The mutilation of the bodies is beyond belief. Doctor Cole's reports makes gruesome reading. Then there is the question of the little statues of the monkeys found on the bodies.'

'What have you found out about that, Sergeant?'

'They first appeared between the 8th and the 17th Centuries. There is a carving over the door of the famous Tosho-gu shrine in Nikko, Japan. The three wise monkeys or three mystic apes, as they were sometimes called, signify a code in gangs or organised crime syndicates that executed people within fifty-nine days.'

'What does that mean, Sergeant?'

'It means, Sir, that these people, who ever they are, may be about to commit another murder. The first two were very close together. That gives them time to commit the third one within the fifty-nine days.'

'Why would anyone want to do that I wonder?'

'That's what we have to find out, Sir, and fast.'

'So where do we go from here, Sergeant?'

'I want to go and interview the friends and relatives of the deceased, see if anything new has come to light. Whoever these people are, Sir, they cover their tracks very well. There isn't much to go on.'

'Okay. I have to go and see the Chief Constable this morning. He's taking a very keen interest in this case. But I still don't have much to tell him.'

As Sergeant Walker passes the front desk, the duty Sergeant calls out to him:

'We had a report last night of a missing person. Before I go home I want to pass it on to CID. Can you look?'

'Yeah, sure. Put it in my tray will you? I'll look at it later. I have more important things at the moment.'

As Neal Shand knocks on the Chief Constable's door, he feels his stomach turning as if he had had a bad curry the night before.

'Come.'

'Morning, Sir.'

'Sit down, DCI Shand.'

'Thank you, Sir.'

'So tell me, what progress have you made so far?'

'Well to be honest, Sir, not much. We have two dead bodies and the only thing linking them are little statues of monkeys.'

'Go on.'

'All we know is that they represent ritual killings of some sort.'

'Yes, I have read the Doctors report. Makes for dreadful reading.'

'Yes, Sir. I've seen the bodies, and I've never seen anything like this in my career. I hope I will never see this again.'

'Please go on, Mr Shand.'

'As I have said, Sir, we don't have much to go on. Sergeant Walker is re-interviewing the victims' families. They couldn't give us much last time. But it's worth a second interview.'

'I see, and?'

'That is about it, Sir.'

'You said these murders were some sort of ritual killing?'

'Yes, Sir, that's right.'

'So tell me more?'

'Well, it's the way the victims were found with these statues of monkeys in their mouths.'

'Tell me what you have found out about that?'

'The story goes back as far as the 8th century Japan. The three wise monkeys or three mystic apes represent three sayings. See no evil, hear no evil, and speak no evil.

'I know the story, Mr Shand, and if I am right, there will be a third murder. Won't there?'

'Yes, Sir. That's what we think.'

'So, where do you go from here? You know there'll be another murder and you must try to stop it, can you?'

'We will try, Sir, but it's not that easy. We just don't have anything to go on. These people, whoever they are, cover their tracks very well. We have no clues.'

'What you mean? Nothing at all?'

'No, Sir, nothing. But I do believe they could be local people.'

'Why do you think that?' asks the Chief sitting at his desk looking at Shand with troubled eyes.

'It's because of the first witness, Miss Christi. She received an anonymous phone call telling her not to talk to the Police.'

'So why does that make them local people?'

'Well, Sir, if they were not I'm sure they wouldn't bother to make threats like that. What I mean is they would be long gone by now and wouldn't care. We have had two identical murders right here in our town. If they weren't local people, why would they come back here to kill?'

'That's for you to find out, Mr Shand.'

'Do we know any locals who would or could do this kind of thing?'

'I've been through our records, Sir. I can't see anyone who could do this. All we have here is petty thefts or a little bit of violence. Fighting outside the Celtic Knot pub on a Saturday night. That kind of stuff, but nothing on this scale.'

'So, Mr Shand, it would seem we have some sort of vigilante group operating in our usually peaceful town, wouldn't it?'

'Yes, Sir, my thoughts exactly.'

'Make this your top priority. I can't have this sort of thing going on here. This is England, DCI Shand, not the Wild West. Do you understand me?'

'Yes, Sir.'

As Neal Shand finally leaves the police station after a long day, the night shift Sergeant comes back on duty.

'Evening, Sir. Long day?'

'Yes, Sergeant, a very long day.'

'Did DS Walker get my report about the missing person?'

'I'm not sure, Sergeant. I haven't seen him all day. He has been out interviewing people. What missing person?'

'Come with me, sir. I'll get the report.

'Here we are. The name's Adrian Jarvis. His Mother called saying he has missed his dinner. I told her we couldn't do much at the moment. But I passed it on to DS Walker before I went off duty this morning.'

'Thank you, Sergeant. I will look into this.'

Molly and Annabel have so much in common despite their difference in age. They are more like sisters these days.

'Tell me about Ireland, will you, Annabel?'

'Oh, it's so beautiful and the people are so friendly and caring. I would love to take you there one day. You would love it.'

'So, why did you leave?'

'Because of a man. He was an Italian from Venice. I met him because he worked near my office. I had a job at the local Gazette. It all seemed to be working out for me until I came home early one day and found him in bed with the sport's mistress from the local school.'

'What a bastard. Why would he do that to you? You're so beautiful?'

'Thank you, Molly. I really don't know. He always seemed to have to prove something to me.'

'What do you mean?'

'Well, he always wanted to be the best lover on earth.'

'And was he?'

Annabel starts to go very red-faced.

'Well, yes, actually he was. But that's not the only thing. There were other things as well. He always wanted to look the best, which was nice when we went out. But he went a little too far. He kept saying I should look better than I did. Always pushing me to dress a little too racy for my taste. I began to feel very uncomfortable. Anyway when I found him in bed with the sport's mistress, that was it for me.'

'You're better off without him. He would never be faithful to you. And my Dad? Tell me?'

'What can I say? The first time we met wasn't a very pleasant time. I found that dead body on the beach'?

'I know. I read about it. It must have been awful.'

'Yes. It was horrible. Your father was so sympathetic and understanding. He made me feel safe. I actually asked him to dinner first.'

'Really? I didn't know that.'

'Yes. He was driving his car one day and stopped to say hello. I just came out with it and asked him to my cottage that same evening.'

'And?'

Annabel giggles. 'And nothing. We had a lovely evening eating and drinking, nothing more. We have been seeing each other ever since. Please tell me you don't mind Molly. He did say he was nervous about telling you because of your mother.'

'Don't worry Annabel. I was a bit worried at first, but not now. I can see how happy he is. My mother is gone and we both have to move on. I will never forget her, but Dad is still young and deserves a new start. And, I've always wanted a big sister.'

Adrian Jarvis cannot tell if it is day or night. He is kept deep into the caves where it is permanently dark, cold and wet. His cries for help go unheard. The rusty old irons around his ankles are starting to cut into him. He does not remember being this scared before. He keeps trying to pull himself free from his chains but they are much too strong and hold him tight. The whisky and the morphine, which helped him forget his condition, have worn off. He slowly realises he is being held prisoner. He is terrified.

The Freohr meet to discuss the next candidate.

'So, when do we do this? We need to get this over with soon.'

'We all agree?'

The rest of the Freohr nod their heads in agreement.

Abrithil stands looking at the others.

'Brethren, I know it's been four days since we imprisoned our candidate in the caves. But I still think it's too soon since the last ceremony. The newspapers still have it on their front pages.'

'We can't hold him forever. We have to finish this now. His mother has reported him missing to the Police, they will be looking for him.'

'All right, tomorrow night, usual time. We'll have to carry out the ceremony in the Smuggler's cave. It's too risky to move him.'

DCI Shand is sitting at his desk re-reading all the paperwork that has been generated since these murders started. Suddenly the phone rings.

'Hello. DCI Shand.'

'Hello, lover. What time will you be picking me up tonight?'

He blushes, thinking to himself how lucky he is.

'Well, I'm not sure. I have a lot of paperwork on my desk and the Chief Constable is breathing down my neck about these murders. Plus, we have another missing person.'

'Really? Who?'

'A local by the name of Adrian Jarvis. He went missing four days ago. His mother reported it.'

'You don't think this could be the next one, do you, Neal?'

' The thought has crossed my mind, Annabel. It does fit with the other crimes. We have everybody looking out for him. But it's a very big area to cover.'

'Okay. Don't worry about tonight. I will take Sherper for a walk, call me on my mobile when you're free.'

'Okay, will do. Bye for now.'

CHAPTER NINE

Since Molly went back to London, Annabel and Neal have been inseparable almost living together full time. Neal loves watching her in the evenings and mornings when she is getting ready for work. He has to force himself to stop looking at her curvaceous figure.

The drive to the police station does not take long but gives him time to reflect on the events so far. He still cannot comprehend what is happening. As he enters his office his assistant is at his desk.

'Sergeant Walker?'

'Yes, Sir?'

'I know you're busy, but I need you to go to the Celtic Knot public house. I want you to re-interview the landlord Harvey Ventura. See what he might remember about our missing person. We believe that was the last place he was seen before he went missing.'

'Straight away, Sir?'

'Yes, straight away please, Sergeant.'

'Shall I take anyone with me, Sir?'

'Yes, Miss Christi wants to go with you. She said she would put something in the local paper, which might help. Pick her up at her office on the way.'

As Sergeant Walker is waiting outside the newspaper office in his car, he sees Annabel Christi walking across the car park. He cannot believe how eye-catching she is, dressed in a light beige jacket and a very short skirt. Her long and very shapely legs seem to go on forever. He whistles to himself thinking, whoa, she looks good.

'Good morning, Miss Christi.'

'Morning, Sergeant. Thank you for picking me up.'

He cannot take his eyes off her legs as she gets into the car. Seeing this she just grins at him.

At the Celtic Knot, Harvey Ventura is working behind the bar, restocking the shelves.

'Mr Ventura, I'm Sergeant Walker, and this is Miss Christi from the local Gazette. I would like to talk to you about Adrian Jarvis.'

'I can't tell you much more than last time, Sergeant. He got very drunk and at some point he left. I didn't see him go.'

He is talking to Sergeant Walker but he is looking at Annabel. She just smiles back at him, crossing her legs and feeling very uncomfortable.

'Please try to think, Mr Ventura. Did he speak to anyone in the bar?'

'No, I don't think so. He wasn't very well liked around here. You know that, don't you? I only let him drink in here out of sympathy. No one really cares if he never comes back. I, for one. He's a customer but a real pain in the arse. He was always upsetting my regular customers.'

'Okay, Mr Ventura. If you do remember anything, you call me, okay? It's extremely important even if he wasn't liked here, he is still a missing person and his mother is worried sick.'

'Okay, Sergeant, will do.'

Ventura turns and speaks to Annabel:

'So, young lady, would you like a drink? On the house of course' He is still looking at her, especially her legs and it is making her feel very self-conscious.

'No, thank you. She turns to look at Sergeant Walker, I think we had better be going.'

'Well, if you ever change your mind gorgeous, I'm always here.'

On the way back in the car Annabel says: 'What a ghastly man. Did you see the way he was looking at me, or should I say leering at me?'

'Yes, I did notice. I can't understand why people go to his pub if that's the way he treats them.'

'Well, I will certainly never go there. That's for sure.'

At this point Walker thinks to himself, now would be a good time to ask her out.

'So, Annabel. I may call you Annabel, my I?'

'Yes, of course, Robert.'

'I was thinking, if you don't want to go to the Celtic Knot for a drink, where would you like to go?'

'Are you asking me out, Sergeant?'

'I suppose I am. Yes, do you mind?'

'No, not at all. Except I am seeing someone, and we are very close. I'm sorry Robert.'

'He's a very lucky man, Annabel. I hope you didn't mind me asking?'

'Not at all. I'm very flattered. You're a handsome man, Robert. If I were single, who knows?'

Back at the Police station, DCI Shand is still at his deck.

'Tell me, Sergeant, what did you find out?'

'Nothing, Sir. Mr Ventura wasn't very forthcoming. He doesn't care about our missing person. He's glad he's missing apparently. Our Mr Jarvis was not liked by any of the locals, they all kept well clear of him.'

'So we are no better off then, are we, Sergeant?'

'Not much, sir, no. We still have nothing to go on. The trouble is these people that have been murdered, and our missing person, were never liked. No one spoke to them. Now the whole town is glad they're gone. They just don't care.'

'I understand, Sergeant. But we still have to try to find the murderers, and our missing person, likeable or not. It's our job.'

' I know, Sir. But it doesn't make our job any easier with no help from the public.'

CHAPTER TEN

As the Freohr are preparing for their next ceremony, one of the Varden speaks:

'Why don't we just let him get washed out to sea?'

Ebrithil answers:

'No we must let the police find him. They have to know why we're doing all this. One day they will understand. It's our duty. Tell the others to begin the ceremony.'

As they walk into the smugglers cave, they can see Adrian Jarvis pulling himself up and tugging at his chains, trying to free himself. He turns round slowly. He cannot believe what he sees. Five men marching towards him all dressed in blood red robes which flap out wide as they walk. The sight and the sound of the deafening sea crashing against the rocks makes Adrian Jarvis shake with a terror he has never experienced before. They stop just short of him and form a circle around him.

'Adrian Jarvis, we have taken you because the Police had to let you go but we know what you're guilty of, and we're going to carry out your sentence. It's the only appropriate sentence. The sentence of death.'

He stands there holding the chains not being able to comprehend what is happening to him. He just looks at these men who are close to him not saying a word with their hands on the hilt of their daggers. Jarvis tries one last time to talk to them. As he pleads for his life, two of the Varden take hold of him. They start cutting all his clothes off leaving him standing there naked and shivering with a combination of cold and extreme terror.

'Look. You've made your point. I'm scared to death. Please let me go and I promise I will never look at any young girls again.'

Ebrithil is staring at him with revulsion in his eyes speaks: 'I'm afraid it's not that simple. You know who some of us are. We cannot let you go now.'

'I won't say a word. I swear on my life,' he shouts.

All of the Varden, stand looking at him with a sneer on their faces, think the same: 'if only you knew how true that last statement is.'

Ebrithil turns to face them, holding his hands out, palms up, saying: 'Brethren begin.'

This time they do not bother gagging their victim because the sound of the sea covers any screams Adrian Jarvis will make. Two of the Varden start to walk towards him slowly, drawing their daggers. The first thrust of the dagger goes straight into his right eyeball. His screams fill the cave. The second one goes to his groin, slicing off his testicles. He nearly faints. Then he feels a knife cutting through the skin on his chest. The pain is so powerful he cannot even scream. His mouth opens but no sound comes out. He is in severe shock. Then the Varden walk away and stand back to form their circle. Next two other Vardens move to take their turn, also drawing their daggers as they move closer. One of them is grinning at Jarvis. This time he takes longer when he thrusts his dagger into the left eye. Slowly in, and slowly out. Twisting it as he pulls it out. Jarvis, although still screaming, can hear only the sound of the waves. Suddenly everything goes black as he falls to the ground.

All the Varden just stand and wait for their victim to bleed to death. However Jarvis still tries to crawl away but the chain becomes taught stopping him. His hands slowly move up his face to feel his eyes but there is nothing there anymore, just two empty holes where they used to be. He then tries to feel his groin but only feels a sticky warm wet substance. The Varden who cut off his testicles also sliced into his penis leaving deep gashes. The mutilation is hideous. The Varden say nothing until Ebrithil breaks the silence saying: 'Finish him now. The tide will wash away the blood.'

All four of them kneel down beside Jarvis stabbing him with a frenzy that was not natural. They seem to go into some sort of trance. Ebrithil has to shout to be heard.

'Enough. Stop. Unchain him and take him to the agreed place.'

This they do without saying a word. Ebrithil just stands there thinking to himself: ' It's the right thing that we do. I'm sure it is.'

CHAPTER ELEVEN

Neal Shand has been summed to the Chief Constables office for the hundredth time this week or so it seems. As he knocks once again on the door, the sound of: 'Come,' puts fear into him. He knows the Chief is pushing to get this murder investigation over as quickly as possible.

'Morning, DCI Shand. What have you got to tell me?'

'Morning, Sir. I'm afraid I still don't have much more to tell you than last time.'

'I understand we have had a missing person report. An Adrian Jarvis. What are you doing about it?'

The Chief is sitting behind his desk staring at Shand with inquiring eyes.

'I have all available officers looking for him, sir. But we have no news yet.'

'Do you think he could be the third victim?'

'We are treating it as that. Sir, yes.'

'How long has he been missing?'

'Four days now, Sir.'

'Does that keep it with the time you told me about, these fifty nine days?'

'Yes, Sir. It does.'

'Okay, Mr Shand. Get on with it and keep me informed with everything you do. Understand?'I mean everything.

'Yes, Sir. Will do.'

As Shand closes the door from the Chiefs office, he lets out a long sigh.

Back in his office, he phones down to the duty Sergeant.

'Any news on our missing person yet?'

'Nothing yet, Sir. We have all available people on it.'

'Okay. Let me know as soon as you hear anything.'

'Will do, Sir.'

He then speaks to Sergeant Walker who instantly answers: 'Yes, Sir.'

'Bring me up to speed on the investigation, please.'

'Well, Sir. Since our last body, we still don't really have much to go on.'

'We must be a little closer surely Sergeant.'

'I'm waiting for the doctor's report. Until then, we haven't got much else. The local people don't seem to care much about our two victims. This is making our investigation extremely difficult, Sir.'

'Understood, Sergeant. But we have to keep digging. Make this last missing person your top priority. Talk to the landlord again. I don't care if we piss him off, we have to get results.'

'Okay, Sir. I'll go back today. Shall I take Miss Christi with me again?'

'I don't think that will be necessary, Sergeant, do you?'

'I guess not. Just a thought.'

Harvey Ventura is washing glasses behind the bar when Sergeant Walker comes through the door. He thinks to himself, they can't have found the body yet. It wasn't meant to be for at least two more days.

'Morning, Mr Walker. What can I get you?'

'Nothing for the moment. I just need another word with you.'

'Where is your lovely assistant today?'

'She's not my assistant. And she won't be coming here anymore.'

'Pity. I could do with a few beautiful women in here like her. It would be good for business.'

'Whatever, now I need to talk to you about Adrian Jarvis. He still hasn't turned up.'

'So what has that got to do with me?'

'This was the last place he was seen in.'

'This is a public house, Sergeant. People come and go all the time. I don't keep track of them. I'm the landlord not their guarding angel.'

'I have just spoken to someone who said they saw a black van in the car park by the back door of your pub, with what they thought to be two men inside. Do you know anyone who owns a vehicle like that?'

'No Sergeant. I don't. Now if you don't mind I have work to do, planning the lunch menu.'

Sergeant Walker says nothing and lets Harvey Ventura walk away. He stands by the bar looking around. He sees a corridor leading to the toilets. He walks over to it and walks down it. He can see the door leading to the car park and the men's room just next to it.

'Seen enough, Sergeant?'
Harvey Ventura is standing behind him. He didn't hear him because he was thinking to himself : 'This Ventura guy is a bit creepy.'

Harvey Ventura is a big man, tall, muscular, with big hands, Sergeant Walker looks at him thinking: 'I wouldn't want to get on the wrong side of you'.

'I was looking for the men's room.'

'I think you found it. Don't you?'

Ventura is pointing to the door with a sign saying 'Men.' He then walks off but looks back and says: 'Have a good day Sergeant.'

Back at the police station Sergeant Walker finds DCI Shand at his desk looking through a mountain of paperwork. He looks up, sees Walker and says:

'Tell me, Sergeant, what have you got for me?'

'Well, sir, Mr Ventura was still very uncooperative. But I do think we could be on to something.'

Shand looks up from his paperwork.

'Go on tell me what have you found out?'

'I got talking to one of the regulars at the Celtic Knot who goes there every day for lunch. He mentioned the day Jarvis was there getting very drunk. He thought it was a bit strange because Ventura was plying him with free whisky.'

'That's very interesting. Go on.'

'Also, he talked about a black van in the car park. He could see it from the men's room window. I checked and you can see out to the car park quite well.'

Shand leans back in his seat looking at Sergeant Walker.

'Well done, Sergeant. This is the first break we've had so far. But did you get anymore on our missing person?'

'No Sir nothing. As I said, Mr Ventura became very disinterested when I mentioned Jarvis' name. I think he knows more than he wants us to believe, Sir.'

'Should we bring him in for a formal interview?'

'Not yet, Sir. But I do think we should have him watched. See where that takes us first.'

'Okay, Sergeant. See to it, I want him watched twenty four hours a day understood? And keep me informed as soon as anything comes up.'

Shand is sitting in his seat staring out the window going over everything Sergeant Walker has just told him when the phone rings, waking him from his trance.

'DCI Shand.'

'Neal, it's Annabel. We have to talk, but not on the phone. Can we meet?'

'What's it about, Annabel? I'm snowed under here.'

'Trust me. I think you will want to hear this. Meet me in the park by the pond. Ten minutes, okay?'

'Okay, but it had better be good. The Chief is jumping down my throat about these murders.'

The walk to the park helps clear Shand's mind. It is a still and warm day just right for a stroll. As he is getting closer to the pond he can see Annabel throwing what looked like bread to the ducks. He still can't believe why she finds him attractive. But he still can't get rid of the feeling of being unfaithful when he thinks about Samantha, his late wife. He feels that he is being disloyal in some way, which he never was all the years they were together. He hopes the feeling will fade away in time.

'Hi. Lovely day.'

'Yes, isn't it?'

'So what's this news that can't wait?'

'I was just on the phone to Sergeant Walker. He mentioned this black van a customer saw the day Adrian Jarvis disappeared.'

'Yes. We had a meeting this morning. He told me he had been back to the Celtic Knot to talk with Mr Ventura, and a black van was mentioned.'

'I think I know where it's parked right now.'

'Did you make a note of the registration number?'

'Err. No, sorry. I didn't think of that.'

'Don't worry. Where is it now?'

'It at the back of the butcher's shop.'

'That's Mr Ambrose's, I think. I don't go there myself. But he has had this shop for thirty years or more. It's normal that he would have a van, don't you think?'

'Yes, I do. But this one is black. There aren't many in this town. I have checked.'

'Okay. Lets go and have a look. I will take the number and run it through the PNC. See what comes up, okay? Anything else?'

'Just that I want you inside me right now.'

Shand blushes bright red. He looks away.

'Annabel, stop it. Someone might hear you.'

They walk nonchalantly past the butcher's shop. Shand makes a mental note of the licence plate and keeps walking. Sure enough, it's black with signs on the side giving the name of the shop. Shand turns to Annabel.

'I can't imagine. If he were involved in some way, would he use this van to kidnap someone? What do you think?'

'You're right. It's a bit strange with the shop's publicity written all over it.'

'As you've made this effort, I will still run the number and see what it brings up.'

'Okay. Will I see you later for dinner?'

'Yes. Who's cooking? You or me?'

'It's Friday, why not let the restaurant do it for us. Shall we?'

'Good idea. I'll pick you up at seven.'

Back at the police station, Shand speaks to the computer operator.

'Run this licence plate for me, would you? And send me any information you get.'

Sitting back at his desk the phone rings. He picks it up.

'DCI Shand.'

'Sir, that number you gave me.'

'Yes. Go on.'

'It belongs to a Mr Arthur Ambrose. He's had the vehicle for two years. He is the first owner. It's registered to his business, the local butcher. There are no outstanding reports on it we have no interest in it, Sir.'

'Okay, thanks. Send up the details, would you please?'

'Will do, Sir.'

Shand sits back in his chair thinking, it was worth a look. There must be two black vans about.

CHAPTER TWELVE

The restaurant is busy. Neal and Annabel have to wait for a table. They are sitting at the bar with a glass of Chablis when Doctor

Cole walks past with his wife.

'Good evening, Mr Shand. We haven't seen you in here before, have we?'

'Evening, Doctor Cole. No I must admit I've only been here once before. Are you a regular here Doctor?'

'Yes. My wife and I come here about once a month. The food is excellent.'

'Must be. It's fully booked tonight. We have to wait at least half an hour for a table.'

'Well, Mr Shand, I hope you enjoy. I'm sure it will be worth the wait.' As he walks away, he nods and smiles at Annabel.

'I know he's a doctor. But he's a bit peculiar, don't' you think?'

'Never really thought about it before, we normally only see each other professionally.'

The meal is worth the wait. Annabel has 'canard à l'orange'. Neal has steak tartar. To complement the food they have an excellent Bordeaux, which was recommended by the headwaiter. As they both start to relax Annabel says:

'When is Molly coming again? I would love to see her.'

'I spoke to her yesterday on the phone. She's up to her eyeballs with studying for her final exams. They are in two months. So I don't think it will be before then.'

'That's a shame. We got on so well.'

'Yes. She told me to say hello to you. Maybe when all this is over we can get away for a break?'

'I would love that, where were you thinking of?'

'I love Spain. You can relax and chillout there. We could swim, snorkel, water ski. But my favourite is to lay on a beautiful sandy beach with the hot sun on my back, and a cold San Miguel in my hand.'

'I like the sound of that. I will have to get a new bikini for the trip.'

'You know they have nudist beaches there. You wouldn't have to worry about a new bikini.'

Annabel slides her hand across the table and takes Neal's hand in hers. She looks into his eyes. He can feel the desire and wanting coming from her.

'That would be fine by me, Neal. But if Molly's coming as well, I think she might have something to say about the two of us lying around completely naked all day, don't you?'

'Hmmm. I guess you're right. Never mind. Maybe, it should be just the two of us. Okay?'

'You can see me naked tonight if you want to. I don't have a sunny, and sandy beach, but I do have a big comfortable bed at home to offer.'

The beam from his face says it all. He calls the waiter for the bill. They walk back to the cottage arm in arm, taking in the lovely warm evening when his mobile rings.

'I don't believe it. Not now, please.'

He looks at Annabel.

'I'm sorry. It's the station. I have to answer it.'

'DCI Shand.'

'Sir, can you come straight away. The chief is asking for you?'

'What have you got?'

'Our missing person has turned up, but you need to see for yourself.'

'Okay, I'm on my way.'

'I'm sorry, Annabel. It sounds serious. I have to go now.'

'Don't worry. I understand. You have a key if you get away. Yes?'

'Yes, I'll be as quick as I can. I promise.'

At the police station Shand talks to the patrol officers who found the body.

'Tell me everything.'

'Sir. We were patrolling along the costal road, when I saw what I first thought was someone swimming. As I got closer I could see the body was naked it was also very obvious the body was in a very bad way.'

'How do you mean?'

'At first, all I could see was that it was covered in blood. It had congealed on the torso. Then as I looked closer, the body had no eyes. And his…'

the police officer starts to tremble with distress, brining his hand up to his mouth.

'Please go on.'

' His testicles were missing.'

'Where is the body now, officer?'

'On the costal road where we found it. There is an officer guarding it. We have called Dr Cole as well.'

'Okay, well done. good work. I know it's not a pretty site. I was present at the last two, so I have an idea what to expect.'

'Who ever did this, Sir are not normal decent people don't do this kind of thing to other people, even if they have a police record.'

'I know, constable. I agree, but these are not normal people we are dealing with.'

As DCI Shand drives to the murder scene he tries to understand. Whoever these people are, why do they have to be so sadistic and brutal to their victims? Even if these people were nasty and cruel it doesn't give them the right to act like this. As he approaches the small viewing point where the murder had taken place he can see Doctor Cole is already there standing over the body talking to the police constable who is keeping guard. Dr Cole looks round as Shand pulls up in his car.

'Evening, Mr Shand. We meet again, did you enjoy your dinner?'

'Evening, Doctor, yes, thank you, It was very nice and we will most certainly go there again. Tell me what do we have here?'

'Well, Mr Shand. It would seem we have our third victim. I have had a look and at first glance it has all the signs of a ritual killing. I will tell you more when I get him to the mortuary.'

'Was there a little statue, Doctor?'

'Yes, Mr Shand. Here, look. I found it in his throat the same as the last two.'

Shand turns it over and over in his hand. It has the inscription '*Lwazaru*' carved on it. Shand thinks to himself: 'so this is the third and last one.'

'Thank you, Doctor. I will call you in the morning when you've had time to examine the body.'

CHAPTER THIRTEEN

As Shand pulls up outside Annabel's cottage, he can see a light in the bedroom and a silhouette by the window. He locks the car and lets himself in. Annabel is standing at the top of the stairs. She looks exquisite in a very skimpy and revealing nightdress. She is smiling at him, a smile that needs no words for him to understand she wants him in her bed now.

He tries to tell her about the body but she puts her finger over his lips and whispers in his ear.

'Tell me in the morning, come to bed.'

Their lovemaking gets more and more passionate each time. The way they explore each other's bodies. Neal loves to caress her breasts slowly, feeling her nipples harden, taking each one in his mouth and sucking them tenderly whilst listening her groan with pleasure. She strokes his penis, which doesn't need much encouragement to become erect. Once they are both excited, their orgasm is the most electrifying experience they have. It is the feeling of being one together. Completely exhausted, they fall asleep in each other's arms.

Over breakfast Annabel asks Neal about the evening before.

'Was it the missing person?'

'Yes, Annabel. It looks like we have our third victim. Doctor Cole has the body and I'll see him later today. But I have to go and tell the Chief first. And what I have to do now is find the people responsible for this, which won't be an easy task.'

'Well, in a strange sort of way, some of the pressure has been taken away now we know there won't be anymore murders.'

'That's one way of looking at it, I guess.'

As Shand pulls up outside the police station, the chief is standing by his car waiting. Shand thinks to himself: 'God, this is all I need first thing in the morning.'

'Morning, Mr Shand. I think we need to talk, my office, ten minutes.'

Shand just looks and smiles at the chief. He enters his office. Sergeant Walker is at his desk, his fingers tapping fast on his keyboard.

'Morning, Sergeant. What have you got for me? I have a meeting with the chief in five minutes. I need to give him good news not bad.'

'I've been on to Doctor Cole but he hasn't had a look at the victim yet. He said he's too busy and can't see to it till this afternoon.'

'So I've got nothing to tell the chief?'

'Well, we are pretty sure it was the third victim of these ritual murders from what the officers' statements describe. Just, that makes for gruesome reading. I can't imagine what Doctor Coles' report will contain.'

'Fair enough, I guess. I will be with the chief if you need me.'

Shand grabs all the paperwork he has on the case and makes his way to the chief's office. He can see the door is open but knocks anyway.

'Come in DCI Shand.'

'Thank you, Sir. I have a statement from the two officers who found the body.'

'Read it to me, please.'

After Shand has finished reading, he can see the chief sitting in his chair hands clasped together in front of his mouth as if in prayer with his eyes closed. Shand gives a little cough to attract his attention.

'Thank you, Mr Shand. I am listing.'

'That's about it for now, Sir.'

'So what do you intend to do next?'

'We still don't have much to go on, Sir.'

'Mr Shand, are you telling me that we have now had three of the most gruesome, macabre, repulsive and horrifying murders I have ever seen or been involved with in my whole police career, and you haven't even got any suspects yet?'

Shand is feeling very uncomfortable, moving in his seat and pulling at his shirt collar, which now feels like it's chocking him slowly.

'As I've said before, Sir, these people have covered their tracks extremely well. We just don't have anything to go on, Sir.'

'You give this case one hundred per cent, understand? Work on this and nothing else. I'm bringing in people from outside to help you.'

'May I ask who, Sir?'

'A criminal psychologist, and a medium.'

'A medium, Sir?'

'Don't knock it, Mr Shand. If these people can help find the guilty party or parties then it's fine with me. We need all the help we can get. Do you understand?'

'Yes, Sir. Of course. Is that it for now, Sir?'

'Yes, for now DCI Shand. But I want daily updates on your progress. Understood?'

'Yes, Sir. Understood.'

Shand walks back to his office his head spinning. He feels as if he cannot breath. The air is too hot for him. He even feels a little light-headed. He stops by an open window and takes a deep breath, trying to calm down after his meeting with the Chief. While he enters his office, Sergeant Walker is sitting at his desk and on the phone. As soon as he puts the receiver down he turns to Shand and asks:

'How did it go with the Chief, Sir?'

'Not good, Sergeant, not good at all.'

'What now, Sir?'

'We are going to be joined by a criminal psychologist and a medium to help find our murderers. We are to give them all the help and intelligence we have.'

'Okay, Sir. I guess it won't hurt, will it?'

'No, DS Walker. It won't hurt at all.'

The only good part of the day will be going home to Annabel's later. He can talk to her easily and openly. She always seems to understand.

After a very long and tiring day, Shand checks his watch. He turns to Sergeant Walker saying: 'Okay, Sergeant, let's go home. All this will still be here tomorrow.'

The drive home always helps Shand to relax, and wind down. He loves to listen to the very distinctive sound of the VW Beetle as it glides along the road.

When enters the cottage, Sherper is waiting by the door with his lead in his mouth and wagging his tail. Shand thinks to himself, what a good idea. A long walk will help to clear my head. He leaves Annabel a note to tell her which way he went if she wanted to join him. They set off up the lane to the cliffs. It is early evening and the sun is setting over the horizon. It looks like a colossal red planet sinking into the sea. He stands there thoughtful while looking at this miraculous planetary phenomenon. How can we live on such a beautiful planet and witness such horrible events such as wars, killings, death, and hatred? He stands there for several minutes deep in thought until he feels a tug on the lead. He looks down at Sherper looking up with an expression in his eyes, which say: 'Let's go.'

CHAPTER FOURTEEN

The Celtic Knot opens at ten in the mornings. Harvey Ventura is getting the till ready for another day when the phone rings. He picks it up still trying to count out the small change.

'Hello. Celtic Knot. How can I help you?'

A voice he knows very well speaks very slowly and clearly.

'We need to meet. We have some unfinished business to take care of.'

He stands there frozen to the spot trying to think what could he mean with 'unfinished business.'

'Okay. Where and when?'

'Tonight, usual time, usual place, be there.'

The phone goes dead.

The same call goes to Arthur Ambrose. Thomas Ackerman, and. Frank de Caux.

That evening they are all waiting, sitting at a large round table. No one says a word. When the door opens two people walk in and sit down. The room is dimly lit with only candles. It is difficult to see even when they are close to each other. Ebrithil stands up and starts to speak:

'Brethren, we are honoured tonight with the presents of the

most adoring grand master of the order of the Freohr.'

All the Varden look at each other trying to see who is in the room with them. All they can see is a figure sitting by Ebrithil with a long black cloak and a hood, which covers his head. He is staring down at the ground. Ebrithil looks round the room smiling at each of the Varden in turn.

'Our work has been very difficult and arduous. But essentially we had a task that needed to be completed. The ceremonies we have accomplished so far have been successful. These horrendous criminals have been removed from society. Our streets are safer now and our children can walk freely. Our Adoring Grand Master has come here tonight to thank you all personally for the work you have carried out.

At this point the Adoring Grand Master stands up still looking down, his hands covered by the wide sleeves on his cloak.

'Brethren. I have come here tonight to show you how grateful I am for all you have done. Two great men, one of who is no longer with us, formed our brotherhood a very long time ago. It is imperative his death is not in vain. We must continue to eliminate these murderers and rapists who escape the law by terrifying their victims into silence because no court convicts them. This is where we come in. We operate above the law and exact our own justice. You were all chosen for individual reasons. Some of you have suffered losses and watched your aggressor walk freely on the same streets as you. Some of you have a hatred for these criminals as much as we all do. Our work carries on because these people continue evading the law.'

The Adoring Grand Master returns to his seat, still looking down keeping his face hidden.

'May I ask Adoring Grand Master? Why did we use the statues of a monkey after each ceremony?'

The Adoring Grand Master still sitting and looking down making it difficult to see him.

'It's our way of showing we are serious in our work. The three wise monkeys are symbols of truth, honesty and justice. The police will have to make up their own minds about this.'

Ebrithil stands up holding out his arms in a gesture of comfort.

'That's all for tonight, Brethren. We will meet again soon. But for now we go about our daily business. And we never speak about our work outside of this circle.'

Both the Adoring Grand Master and Ebrithil stand up and walk out of the room. The rest of the Varden have to wait till they were nowhere to be seen. Then they move away slowly not speaking a word to each other.

CHAPTER FIFTEEN

Shand is at his desk very early before any of the other team has arrived. He is shifting through what looks like a growing mountain of paperwork. Sergeant Walker enters with a cup of coffee in his hand. He sees Shand sitting at his desk.

'Morning, Sir. You're early this morning.'

'Morning, Sergeant. Yes, I wanted to get a head start before these people arrive.'

'Which people, Sir?'

'You remember, the Chief is bringing in a psychologist and a medium?'

'Oh, yes, I remember now. What time are they coming?'

'About nine. I think we need to be ready before they get here.'

At nine sharp Shand's office phone rings.

'DCI Shand.'

'Front desk, Sir. I have a Doctor Simmonds and a Miss Collins, to see you.'

'Okay, I'll send Sergeant Walker down to collect them. Five minutes. Okay?'

As Shand puts the phone down he looks at Sergeant Walker.

'Would you mind Robert? 'They're here downstairs in the front office.

'Of course, Sir. On my way.'

As Sergeant Walker is making his way down to the front reception area he thinks to himself: 'that's the first time he's ever used my first name. He must be really worried about this case.' He returns to the office and introduces the guests.

'Sir, this is Miss Collins. She is the medium. And this is

Doctor Simmonds, the psychologist.'

Shand stands up and offers his hand to both of them in turn. He notices that Doctor Simmonds has an unusually strong hand shake for a man that looks somewhere in his late sixties, albeit a tall man, quiet slim with a haggard face and a mop of white hair. Miss Collins who he estimates at between forty and forty five years old has a vagueness about her as if she is thinking about something completely different. It is difficult to see her form as she is wearing a long black cloak that sweeps the floor when she walks.

'I'm pleased to meet you both. Please take a seat and I'll run you through the proceedings so far.'

They sit down. Doctor Simmonds takes out a note pad and a pencil. Miss Collins is still looking a bit elusive. Shand holds direct eye contact but can't seem to get much of a reaction from her. Once he has explained the case so far in minute detail he sits back in his chair waiting for a reaction. Doctor Simmonds is the first to speak.

'So with three dead bodies who have been murdered in a most peculiar and macabre way, a very detailed coroner's report to help you, you still have no suspects. Am I right?'

'Yes, Doctor, that's about it. I have been ordered by the Chief to give you all the help and assistance I can. But please remember the reason you are both here is to offer us all the help and assistance we need. Do we understand each other?'

'Completely Mr Shand, absolutely, completely. I'm just trying to make some sort of sense of it. I've never come across anything of this kind before'

Shand leans forward and asks both of them.

'Have you had a look at the bodies yet?'

'Yes, Mr Shand we did yesterday. The Chief was most insistent that we went to the mortuary before we saw you.'

'And as a psychologist what kind of people do you think could commit such a monstrous crime?'

'Just because these three were murdered in such a hideous way doesn't automatically mean the murderers are mad or if they firmly believe they were doing this for some kind of ultimate goal. By this I mean they strongly believed that they were actually doing good in a bizarre way. A type of cleansing process. Look back in history at Hitler, Mr Shand. He had this abnormal hatred for Jews and homosexuals. It's said he genuinely thought he was doing good for mankind by trying to eliminate them.'

The conversation carried on for quite a long time, when all of a sudden Miss Collins stands up and cuts into the conversation.

'The Castle.'

Shand, Walker and Dr Simmonds, all stand up and look at her, then at each other. Miss Collins is standing looking out of the window; still with this vague look in her eyes, she speaks again holding her arm out pointing with a long bony finger.

'The Castle. We must go there now.'

Shand grabs the phone on his desk.

'This is DCI Shand. Get the team ready to move in one minute and have my car waiting with a driver, we are on our way down. Sergeant Walker, take Doctor Simmonds with you please and

Miss Collins with me, please.'

They all run down to the car park where the forensic team are waiting together with an armed unit on the Chiefs orders. The drive to the Castle seems to take for ever Shand keeps looking at his watch, he turns to his driver.

'Come on Jim put your foot down, we don't have all day.'

'Right you are, Sir.' A big grin appears on his face as he feels the Police pursuit car accelerating harder.

When they eventually get to the parking, the other units are already waiting. Shand calls them all together to brief them. 'We know the Castle has been out of bounds for at least two years because of structural damage, so watch your step. I'll go in first with Miss Collins, do nothing till I signal. This could be a crime scene. I don't want anything disturbed understood?'

Shand and Miss Collins walk off heading into the Castle grounds. She keeps stopping and looking around not saying a word, Shand thinks he can see her lips moving as if she is talking to someone. She moves off again this time touching parts of the stone walls, running her hands over them as if she was caressing them like some sort of lover, she walks very slowly to the centre of the castle grounds and stops. She looks up to the sky, then down to the ground, again Shand sees her lips moving. She then puts her arms around herself as if she is cold. She starts to sway from side to side. Now Shand can hear her chanting something except he can't quite make it out. She turns to Shand and looks straight into his eyes with a stare that sends a shiver down his spine. He feels the hairs on his neck rising. The wind is gusting and shrieking within the stone walls making her long hair fly up, over her face, however, she doesn't bother to brush it away she appears completely lost in her own world. Then with one hand she very slowly extends her long, bony, index finger and points to Shand. Her stare feels like it is cutting into him, she points downward to a large flat stone on the ground.

'There.'

Shand looks at her, then down at the stone.

'What is it? What do you mean?'

'That stone, this is where it happened, this is where the murder took place,' she talking still pointing at the stone and looking absorbedly down at the ground.

Shand is a little lost for words; he's not sure what to do next, he has never experienced this kind of thing before. Nevertheless, he takes his police radio out of his jacket and starts speaking.

'Bring the forensic team in, we have something here.'

He turns to Miss Collins who is still looking around the area.

'How sure are you that this is the place?' he asks.

She looks into his eyes again with a penetrating cold look.

'He told me.'

'Who told you, what?'

'The deceased, Mark Bruley. He just spoke to me.'

The forensic team arrive, walk past him and start setting up their equipment.

Shand still cannot believe what he has just heard. He feels like he is elevating above everybody and looking down.

'Miss Collins, can you sense anything else?

'Yes, Mr Shand, this was not the only murder that took place here, there was another. Shand is starting to feel stupid asking these questions but if it brings results why not.

'Miss Collins, I need you to tell me everything you know. It's extremely important.'

'When the deceased decide to talk to me Mr Shand, I will communicate to you what they say.'

Shand needs to get away from the murder scene and think about what he has just experienced. It is all too much for him, he calls over his Sergeant.

'Sergeant Walker, stay here and tell me what forensics find. I'm going back to the police station to talk to the Chief, and keep an eye on Miss Collins.'

'Right you are, Sir, leave it to me.'

CHAPTER SIXTEEN

Shand's brain is still racing at a hundred miles an hour as he walks into his office. He pours himself a coffee. His hands are trembling, trying to pour it out. He puts the pot down and sits at his desk. The phone rings shaking him from his thoughts. He picks up the receiver slowly and puts it to his ear, all he hears is.

' Detective Chief Inspector Shand. My office now, please.' the phone goes dead.

He is sitting there, at his desk, still with the receiver in his hand looking at it. Eventually he puts the phone down, slowly stands up, takes a deep breath and walks to the Chiefs office. He knocks lightly on the door.

'Come.'

'Morning, Sir.'

'Come in, Mr Shand. Sit down and tell me what is going on at the Castle?'

'Well, Sir. It's difficult to know where to start.'

'I always find the beginning is a good place, Mr Shand.'

Shand definitely feels either sarcasm or anger in the Chief's voice. It is difficult to tell which one. He is standing with his back to him, looking out of the window.

Shand coughs to give him time to compose himself.

'I'm waiting, Mr Shand.'

The Chief then turns round and sits at his desk moving his hands to his favourite position as if in prayer. This tells Shand it is time to start with his briefing.

'We went to the Castle on the advice of Miss Collins. I went inside first with her. She seemed to go into some sort of trance as if she was talking to someone. Except I couldn't hear anything. Then all of a sudden she pointed to a large flat stone and said: 'There. This is where the murder took place.' That's about it for the moment, Sir.'

'What did you do then?'

'I called in forensics. They're still there now with Sergeant Walker and Miss Collins. I came back here to brief you, Sir.'

'Well done, Mr Shand. This is the best lead we have had so far, stick with it.'

'Yes, Sir. There is more. She also said that there was more than one murder that took place at that spot.'

'Do you mean we have found the place for all three murders?'

'I'm not sure yet, Sir. All she said was there was another, we will have to wait and see what forensics come up with.'

'If that's all, Mr Shand, you had better get on with it, keep me posted of any and all events. Do you understand?'

Back in his office he pours himself a coffee with no problem, the trembling hands are fine now. He sits at his desk just as the phone rings, startling him back to life.

'DCI Shand.'

'Neal, it's Annabel. I've just heard about what's going on at the Castle, why didn't you tell me?'

'Annabel, I'm sorry. I couldn't talk about it until I was sure we had something, come to my office now I'll take you with me, I'm going back shortly okay?'

'Okay. I'll be there in ten minutes.'

On the drive down Neal explains every detail to Annabel; of the events that had happened so far; even about Miss Collins talking to the deceased.

'Do you believe in all this medium talking to dead people stuff, Neal?'

'Before today I would have said no. But after what I experienced in my office this morning and at the Castle, I have to say that I'm not sure anymore, there's definitely something in it, all I know is it shook me up. I've never had any contact with people like this before.'

'Can any evidence she gives be used in court?'

'Again Annabel, I can't be certain. A good lawyer would have a field day with this, all I do know is, if forensics come up with solid proof that the murders took place there, we will be much closer to finding the people responsible.'

As they arrive at the parking there is a hive of activity with the police and forensics in action. Annabel looks into the Castle and asks Neal:

'Is that her over there with the long black cloak on?'

'Yes, that's Miss Collins.'

'Can I talk to her?'

'Yes, but you must tell me everything she says, okay?'

Annabel walks across to where Miss Collins is standing. She is still caressing the walls and talking to herself. It's more like some sort of chanting than talking.

'Miss Collins, I'm Annabel Christi from the Local Gazette. DCI Shand said it would be all right to talk to you, do you feel up to answering some questions?'

'I'm fine, Miss Christi. I wasn't the one murdered here. He

was.'

She's looking over to the far side of the Castle pointing to a small inlet in the walls where tourists used to sit to admire the view. Annabel is taken aback by Miss Collins calmness. She seemed to be taking it all in her stride.

'Miss Collins, what do you mean? He was?'

'Mark Bruley. He's standing over there. I've been talking to him.'

Annabel looks across as if she expected to see Mark Bruley standing there talking to the police. All she sees are old cracked stonewalls, she looks back at Miss Collins and smiles. Miss Collins grins back but it's more a skeptical kind of smile than a happy one.

'Have you ever had contact with the dead, Miss Christi?'

'No. Never I'm afraid.'

'Then let me enlighten you. I am a medium, I didn't ask to be one, I don't think any of us do, it just happens, some people call it a gift, I call it a curse. The point is the deceased contact me if they believe they have been taken before their time, in an unjustifiable way or, if they want to make contact with a loved one to reassure them that they're okay and shouldn't worry about them even though they have passed over, do you understand?'

'I understand the principals behind it, but not the feasibility, this is my first experience of this kind of thing.'

'Then don't dismiss what you don't understand, Miss Christi. When I said he is standing over there, I can see him, you can't. I can talk to him, you can't he dosen't want to talk to you. He chose me because of my powers and ability to connect with him. He wants his executioners brought to justice, he admits he did wrong but he doesn't understand why his death had to be so violent, and hideously painful.'

'Tell me please, what did he say?'

'He said he was taken prisoner, he can't remember for how long, he was bound with strong nylon rope that cut into his wrists, he had a rag pushed into his mouth that tasted of vinegar, he was stripped naked. The next thing he remembers is that he was brought here one night, there were five men all dressed in blood red robes standing around him in a circle chanting some kind of ritual, then one of them walked towards him grinning.'

'I'm sorry to interrupt, Miss Collins. How do you mean grinning? This man was about to kill him how can he be grinning?'

'All I know, Miss Christi is what Mark Bruley told me, shall I carry on?'

'Yes, sorry, please go on Miss Collins.'

'As I was saying, this man was smiling or grinning at him, then very fast he pushed something into his eye and gouged it out, equally as fast, he gouged out the other eye, before he could try to understand what had just happened another man walked up to him and pushed something into his mouth and started pulling out his tongue, but this time he did it gradually, he was also smiling or grinning while doing this, he remembers passing out but at some time he was brought back to conciseness, and the unbearable pain continued for what seemed like an eternity, then he remembers nothing. That must have been the moment of death.'

Annabel is starting to feel physically sick, she places her hand over her mouth and turns away from Miss Collins. Neal is walking over to her and sees she is in some kind of distress.

'Are you all right, Annabel?'

'Miss Collins has just described what happened here. It was hideous I thought I was going to throw up.'

'Let's go. Forensic has finished and we are going to cordon the area off. I'm leaving a police officer here overnight. They want to come back in the morning. They seem to think they will find more.'

Miss Collins looks up and straight at Shand.

'They will find a lot of horror here, Mr Shand. Some very evil and dark things have happened here. Mark Bruley wasn't the only one.'

'Yes, Miss Collins. I'm beginning to understand. I'd like to see you in my office first thing tomorrow if that's all right?'

Later that night, both Neal and Annabel have problems sleeping, they are laying awake, heads spinning, going over and over the events of the day, eventually they drift off and the next thing they hear is the alarm ringing. Annabel gets up first and showers while Neal is making the coffee, when she has finished she walks into the kitchen with just a towel around her, her flaming red wet hair brushed back over her head showing her face completely. Neal looks up and sees her standing there and thinks to himself: 'She is so beautiful, what a lucky man I am.'

'Are you coming to the police station with me this morning, Annabel?'

'Yes. I called my editor and he said to make this my top priority, this is the biggest thing to hit these parts for a long time, probably ever.'

'That's exactly what the Chief is saying as well.'

After breakfast they both climb into Neal's VW Beetle. The drive to the police station is very quiet, they are both in deep thought, as he is parking the car he sees Miss Collins and Doctor Simmonds walking into the reception area of the police station, they both sit in the car for a moment enjoying the peace and quiet, looking at each other. Annabel speaks first.

'What do you think today will bring? will you find the people that did this?'

'I'm not sure about that, but I do think we are a lot closer now we have a murder scene, let us go and see what the good Doctor Simmonds has to tell us, shall we?'

In the briefing room everybody is gathered, including the Chief, Doctor Cole, the forensic scientist and Miss Collins. Shand stands up and introduces himself. He then makes sure everyone knows who everyone else in the room as they all have a vital role to play. He sits down letting the forensic doctor talk about what he has found.

'Morning, everybody. I'm the head of the forensic team on this case, I want to tell you what we found yesterday, thanks to Miss Collins who led us there, I can confirm that the Castle was the scene of the murder, the forensics we gathered, matched with the deceased, leaves us with no doubt we are in the right place.'

Doctor Cole looks round the room. 'You said 'murder' as in one. I happen to know that there were three murders, am I right?'

The forensic doctor stands up looks at Doctor Cole with a little surprise.

'Yes, Doctor Cole. I did say 'murder.' No one has said anything about more than one at the Castle, as far as I know this information is classified for now.'

The Chief stands up, holds up his hand to gesture quiet.

'Gentlemen, please, let's not get crossed wires here, we have a murder scene, we have three dead bodies, all we need to do now is match them to the scene, surely?'

He is looking at the forensic doctor for confirmation. The doctor is checking his notes whilst talking to a colleague, he looks up at the Chief.

'I can't be sure yet, but we did find other traces of blood that didn't match the deceased Mark Bruley. We are still checking this. Miss Collins said there was more than one murder at the Castle, so we still have a lot of work to do.'

The Chief stands up again. 'Miss Collins, would you please tell all of us what you experienced at the Castle yesterday?'

Miss Collins stands up very slowly looking round the room. It appears she is not comfortable with this kind of situation.

'All I can tell you is I spoke with the deceased, Mark Bruley yesterday at the Castle, it was he who called me there, he told me about his murder and how it happened. I passed this onto the police and Miss Christi. I would rather not go over it again, it disturbs me greatly, just because I have the ability to talk to the deceased doesn't mean I enjoy it.'

Shand stands up to take control of the meeting. 'Thank you Miss Collins, we really do appreciate your help in this case.'

Shand feels really stupid asking this but he has to.

'Miss Collins, did Mr Bruley mention another victim?

'No, he said nothing about anyone else.'

'All right then, did he talk about the people that did this to him?'

'All he said was there were five men all dressed in blood red robes with long daggers hanging from a wide black belt. I asked if he could see their faces but he didn't answer, he is still in a lot of pain, even after someone has passed over to the other side, they can still have feelings.'

'Thank you Miss Collins.'

'Now before we move to the murder scene, I would like to hear what Doctor Simmonds has to offer?'

'I have studied the evidence so far and what Miss Collins has told me. My professional opinion is these individuals, who ever they are, firmly believe they are doing something good by getting rid of these people they feel don't fit into society, people that commit heinous crimes. So these individuals could be anyone living in this town or surrounding areas, they are people just like us in this room going about their daily lives without any kind of remorse about murdering fellow human beings. They are unlikely to change since they don't see any reason to do so. It's a very difficult medical condition to diagnose even in my field of study. What we need to do is find one of them at least so I can analyze him, until then there is not much more I can offer to this case.'

'Thank you, Doctor Simmonds, unless there are anymore questions I propose we move on,' suggests Shand.

Doctor Cole stands up glaring straight into Doctor Simmonds eyes, pointing a finger at him and starting to talk without being asked.

'What gives you the right to stand here this morning and be so sanctimonious about this case? You don't live in this town, you don't know the people that live here, you don't know the kind of scum we have to put up with on our streets, watching them on a daily basis as if they have nothing to worry about and in the full knowledge they are above the law, we have to breath the same air as these people. It makes me sick to the stomach just to look at them.'

Shand stands quickly to interrupt and quieten things down.

'Thank you, Doctor Cole, for your opinion, we will make note of your feelings.'

Back in his office Shand pours himself a coffee, he looks at his hand but it is not shaking. Sergeant Walker follows him in also pouring out a coffee for himself. Shand looks at him.
'Robert.'
'Yes, Sir, what can I do for you?'
'That little outburst from Doctor Cole…'

'Yes, Sir, it struck me as a bit odd.'

'I'm not happy the way he reacted to Doctor Simmonds. It was a bit too personal for my liking. I want you to check him out. I mean thoroughly, go back as far as you can, do you understand?'

'Yes, Sir. I'll start straight away, but don't you need me at the murder scene?'

'Yes, I do, but this is just as important. I hope I'm wrong. I really do.'

The phone rings on Shand's desk, he picks up the receiver, he hears the Chief.

'Mr Shand, you're still here? Good, can you pop up to my office now, please?'

As Shand walks into the Chief's office he sees him standing looking out of the window hands crossed behind his back.

'Sir, you wanted to see me?'

'Yes, Mr Shand I did. I'm a little concerned with Doctor Cole's outburst just now.'

'Me too, Sir, so concerned I've ordered Sergeant Walker to do a full investigation on him.'

'Do you think that's really necessary?'

'Yes, Sir, I do. In light of what I have learned recently, as far as I'm concerned, everyone is a suspect until proven otherwise.'

'I'm glad to see you're being so meticulous in your work, Mr Shand. I'll leave you to it.'

As Shand moves to the door to leave, the Chief turns to face him.

'Am I on your list of suspects, Mr Shand?'

'Like I said, Sir, everyone is, until proven otherwise.'

CHAPTER SEVENTEEN

Even on a bright and sunny day the Castle seems a bit eerie, even more now it is a murder scene. Shand is standing next to Miss Collins who still has this impenetrable look about her as if she is somewhere else. He sees the forensic team packing up their things and walks over to the head of the team.

'Have you finished your investigation already?'

'Yes, Mr Shand. We have just about everything we can get from here. But please keep it cordoned off; we might have to come back at sometime. Try not to let anyone walk over this spot, it's still a murder scene.'

Shand walks back to Miss Collins he tells her.

'They're leaving. They have all they need for now. Is there anything more you can tell me, Miss Collins?'

'No, I'm sorry, nothing. He didn't come today.'

'Mark Bruley, you mean?'

'Yes. They don't make contact on a regular basis. Sometimes they are reluctant to talk. I have to encourage them to speak.'

Shand looks at her still not really sure if he believes what she is telling him.

'Okay, let's get back to the police station. I will have an officer take a statement from you, then you can go.'

Clancy Belet is sitting at his desk at the bank where he has been the manager for the last fifteen years. He is forty-eight but already twice divorced, the first time because he was starting to show violent tendencies towards his wife. She walked out on him. His second wife also walked out when their daughter was violently raped by a gang of boys for which he did nothing. He just blocked it out and never spoke about it to anyone.

His mobile phone rings, which is unusual during the day as everyone calls him on his office phone. He sees who is calling.

'Why are you calling me on my mobile?'

A voice he knows well replies with an icy and hostile tone.

'The police have found out about the Castle. They have strong DNA evidence of what happened there.'

'How did they find out? You said that could never happen.'

There is a tremble in Clancy Belet's voice. He sounds scared and worried. He pulls a handkerchief from his pocket and dabs his forehead.

'The police hired a medium. She told them where to go. She said she had contact with Mark Bruley who told her everything.'

'Jesus Christ, we're lost. The police will be coming for us. We have to escape now.'

'Calm down. I said they found the Castle. They still have no idea who we are, apparently Mark Bruley didn't talk about us.'

'I don't like this. I don't like this at all. What are we going to do?'

'We carry on. Our work is not finished. The Grand Master wants us to continue.'

'How can we? We have finished with the three Monkeys. There can be no more, can there?'

'Look into your Japanese history brother. I'll be in touch.'

The phone goes dead. Clancy Belet sits at his desk staring at his phone not believing what he just heard.

Annabel and Neal are having dinner. It's been another very long day. She turns to him and asks.

'Did the forensic team find anything else at the Castle?'

'Yes they found traces of another blood type. We have to trace it and see if it fits one of the other victims.'

'This is really very disturbing stuff Neal, don't you think?'

'Well, it's undoubtedly different to anything I've been involved in before.'

Annabel looks at him with her big engaging eyes.

'What are you thinking, Annabel?'

'Just looking, Neal, just looking. Why don't we try to forget about all this for one night?'

'So, what are you thinking?'

She walks around the table, stops, bends over him. Her face is next to his; he feels her breath on his cheek. She kisses him softly on his lips, her tongue slipping into his mouth. Then she takes his hands in hers.

'Come with me and I'll soothe all your worries away.'

Annabel leads him to the sofa makes him sit down, she then puts on some slow easy listening music and starts dancing in front of him. Swaying her hips from side to side, moving her hands over her body very slowly, caressing herself. She looks at Neal with a smile, and very seductively and gradually she lifts her top to show her shapely breasts pulling it over her head and throwing it onto the floor. Then she turns her back to him still gyrating her hips. Very slowly she releases her bra and lets it drop to the floor. At the same time she undoes the zip on her skirt pulling it down. She turns her head to look at Neal she is looking passionately at her. She is just in her camiknickers now. She turns back to him; he still cannot believe how exquisite in every way she is. Her firm breasts, flat stomach, long shapely legs, she holds out her hands as if to say: 'come to me now.' Neal feels his erection pushing in his trousers. It is clear he is very excited by the way Annabel aroused him.

'Wow, is all that for me? I'm a lucky girl. What did I do to deserve all this?'

He actually feels a little shy. He is not sure what to say. He feels like a little boy who has been caught playing with himself. She undoes his zip and lets his trousers fall to the floor. He kicks them away. She pulls off his shirt urgently, gently biting him on the shoulder. He takes Annabel in his strong powerful arms, pulling her to him and kissing her full lips fervently, his tongue frenziedly searching in her mouth. She wriggles in his arms to get closer to his erection, pushing herself to him. At the same time her hands follow his muscular chest and stomach down to his boxer shorts, which she pulls down. Neal then moves his head down to her breasts, starts licking one nipple then the other, making them more erect. She moans, throws her head and shoulders back to show her breasts completely to him. She tugs at his underwear. He helps her by pulling them off. He is standing in front of her entirely naked with the most powerful erection she has ever seen. She takes his penis in her hand and softly strokes it up and down. He sighs with pleasure. He then pulls her Camiknickers off frantically. They are now both completely naked, standing in front of each other, fondling and kissing, exploring each other's bodies. Neal moves his hand between her legs and caresses her. He feels she is moist and eager for his erection to enter her as she pushes herself to him. She jerks her head back to look at him.

'Take me now, Neal, right here on the carpet.'

He carries her gently to the rug in front of the fire. He stands for a moment looking at her, taking in the full exquisiteness of her body. She holds out her arms telling him to come to her. He lowers himself to her, she opens her legs a little just enough for him to enter her. She cries out with pleasure as he thrusts deep inside her. They make love, caressing each other, kissing each other. With every stroke he drives into her she moans with pleasure looking up at him beaming. He can hear her whisper.

'Deeper, Neal, deeper. Faster, Neal, faster. I can feel you inside me.' As their lovemaking gets more and more intense, her fingernails dig into his back. They both climax at the same time, crying out. Neal lowers himself onto her panting. Annabel, her eyes closed, licks her lips, moving her head side to side. Slowly she opens her eyes and looks up at him.

'Thank you. You are magnificent.'

Neal looks down at her, kisses her with a passion he didn't know he had. They are both covered in sweat. He can see the sweat between her breasts, kisses her there still fondling her.

'I think you're loosing your erection. Will you get another one for me soon?

Neal laughs. He loves the way she looks, laying there naked, sweaty, glowing, and fully contented.

'I will most certainly try.'

They come down to breakfast the next morning. Neal looks at the table.

'What a mess, we didn't clear away last night.'

Annabel puts her arms around him, resting her head on his shoulder.

'We had better things to do last night than the washing up, remember?'

He blushes, thinking about last night.

'Oh, yes, I remember, How could I forget.'

As Annabel is getting the breakfast ready the phone rings. It is Molly.

'Hi, dad.'

'Hello, darling how are you?'

'I'm fine. What's all this I've been reading in the newspapers?'

'I know, it's bad, but we are making progress. It's not the usual kind of thing we get down here. Are you coming to see me?'

'Yes, I have some time off. I was thinking of getting the train today. I could be there by eight tonight. I know it's short notice but what do you think?'

'I think that would be wonderful. I can't wait to see you.'

'Okay. Can you meet me at the station?'

'I'm not sure, darling I'm really busy with what's been going on here, but if I can't Annabel will be there, is that okay?'

'Yes, perfect. I can't wait to see her again.'

'Okay, see you later tonight then. Bye for now.'

Annabel walks into the living room carrying a tray with two coffee cups.

'Was that Molly?'

'Yes, she's coming down tonight. Can you pick her up at the station?'

'Of course, I would love to.'

CHAPTER EIGHTEEN

The drive to the police station is always a calm moment for Neal; it gives him time to think about all the recent events, also about the events of last night with Annabel. This brings a big smile to his face. As he approaches his parking spot he sees the chief standing talking to the press just outside the front door on the steps. He parks his car and walks slowly to the crowd that has gathered. The chief introduces him.

'This is detective chief inspector Shand. He is in charge of the investigation.'

The chief turns to him and whispers softly in his ear: 'Where the hell have you been, we have another missing person?'

He looks at the chief then to the press reporters, back to the chief with surprise in his eyes; he can't believe what he's hearing.

'What? When did this happen?'

'Apparently it was about 3 a.m. his morning, somebody called the station and reported it.'

'Sir, I can't talk to the press now. I have no information about this new case. Can you handle them for me, please?'

'Of course, Shand. Leave it to me.'

'Alright ladies and gentlemen that's all for now. I will give a press release later today.'

Both Shand and the chief walk into the station. He still cannot believe what he has heard. His head is spinning with the thought of it all. He turns to the chief.

'Is this latest missing person related to the case?'

The chief turns to look at him. He has disapproval in his eyes.

'Mr Shand, I thought you had this case under control and that we were moving forward with the finding of the murder scene, at least for two of them. And now it would seem it's starting again. Can you explain it to me, please?'

Shand is totally shocked he does not know where to look. For the first time in his career he feels incredibly lost.

'First, I need to speak to the person who reported it. Then I'll have more to go on.'

'Do that, Mr Shand. Do it now.'

Shand runs to his office, picks up the phone and speaks to the duty sergeant.

'This is Detective Chief Inspector Shand. What have you got on this latest missing person?'

'All I've got, Sir, is a call. It came in last night about 3 a.m. someone saying that his or her son wasn't in his bed. They were told by the night sergeant to call again this morning if he was still missing.'

'Send everything up to my office, please.'

Shand walks to the coffee machine to pour himself a cup. As he picks up the percolator his hands are shaking. He thinks to himself: 'shit not again.'

The sergeant knocks on his door with the report from last night.

'This it for now, Sir. Not much to go on, I'm afraid.'

Shand looks at the report, and all he sees is the name of the person who called. Her name is Mrs Winter and her son's is Daniel

Winter. He makes a note of the address as gathers his things together. Sergeant Walker walks into the office.

'Morning, Sir. You look worried.'

'You can say that, Sergeant. We have another missing person. Come with me.'

Sergeant Walker's jaw drops and his eyes open wide.

'What? How? When? Where?'

'That's what we need to find out and fast. Get the car ready, we are going to see Mrs Winter.'

As they pull up outside the house, Shand can see the curtains moving. They walk to the front door. It opens before they reach it. Mrs Winter comes to the door crying.

'Are you the police?

'Yes, Mrs Winter, I'm DCI. Shand and this is DS Walker. Can we come in?'

She leads them into the living room.

'Please sit down. Would you like some tea?'

'No, thank you. Not now. Please tell us why you think your son is missing?'

'Well, he went out last night to see some friends. He said he would be back by midnight. I waited up for him. So when he wasn't back by three I called the police.'

'Mrs Winter, we need to know who your son was going to meet?'

'He never told me, he just said he was meeting some friends in the park.'

117

'Do you have any idea who? It's extremely important.'

'Well, one of them was called Tony, I think. No, wait a minute. It wasn't Tony. It was Tom. Yes, that's it. Tom.'

'Tom who, Mrs Winter? Please try to remember.'

She is sitting in an old armchair biting her fingernails staring at the floor deep in thought. Shand and Walker look at each other. Shand looks around the room, it is full of old furniture, with threadbare rugs on a dusty wooden floor and long dark curtains hide old filthy windows. The walls are covered with family photos. A clock is ticking somewhere behind him.

'Tom Carter. Yes that's it. I'm sure. Tom Carter.'

'Okay Mrs Winter, well done. Do you have any idea where we can find this Tom? We need to talk to him as soon as possible.'

'I have no idea. I'm sorry. I never knew where he lived.'

'Don't worry, Mrs Winter. If we know him, we can find him. In the mean time if you think of anything else that will help us please call the police station immediately. Okay?'

'Yes, I will. I promise. Please find him for me.'

'We will do our best, Mrs Winter. Goodbye for now.'

On the drive back to the police station Shand asks his Sergeant: 'What did you find out about our Dr Cole?'

'Nothing, Sir. Absolutely nothing. He's squeaky clean, not even a parking ticket. As far as the police are concerned he doesn't exist.'

'So we can assume his little outburst was just that? He really must love his job and his hometown. Don't bother looking any further. We have more important things to worry about.'

Back at the police station Walker runs the name Tom Carter through the police computer. He gets an address. Up in his office he tells Shand what he has found.

'Sir, we have an address on Tom Carter. It's local. Shall I go and have a word?'

'Yes, but I'm coming as well. I'm sorry, Robert, but if this is another potential murder I have to be there. You understand don't you?'

'Of course, Sir, no problem. Let's go.'

The address takes them to a run down council estate on the outskirts of town, which looks like a war zone. There are burnt out cars on the street curbs, rubbish everywhere, gangs of boys hanging around on street corners smoking and drinking out of cans that look like strong beer. They look at Shand and Walker with wariness as they drive past. When Walker looks back at them, they quickly hide something from them pushing what ever it is back into rucksacks lying on the ground. Walker turns to Shand.

'This reminds me of that film 'Escape from New York.' All we need now is Snake Plissken jumping over that burnt out car, firing his machine gun, dragging the President behind him.'

Shand looks at Walker smiling, forgetting for a moment why they are there.

'Now, now Sergeant Walker, it's not as bad as that. Not yet anyway.'

They find the house they are looking for in a small cul-desac. It looks like it has not seen paint since the day it was built. There are dirty stained curtains on even dirtier cracked windows. The garden has an old motorbike with the front wheel missing and most of the engine on the grass. The front door has no bell; they have to bang with their fists to make themselves heard. Eventually they can hear footsteps from inside, the door opens slowly creaking like an old castle door. A man's face appears, a cigarette in his mouth and a dishevelled beard of at least three days growth on his face. He is dressed in an unwashed white t-shirt with a picture of Nelson Mandela on it and covered with food stains. The blue jeans are ripped at the knees and covered in grease. He is wearing no shoes or socks, showing long black toenails.

'Yeah? What do you want? Who are you?'

'Mr Carter?'

'Yeah. That's me. So what?'

'I'm DCI Shand and this is my colleague D. Walker. Can we come in?'

'What for? I ain't done nothing wrong?'

'We didn't say you have. We just want to talk to you, that's all.'

'All right then. I guess it's okay. Come in.'

Shand and Walker walk along the hallway into the living room. The dirt is unbelievable. There is a very strange smell coming from somewhere. They both look at the furniture and think to themselves: ' if I sit there, I'll never get up again. God only knows what's living in there.

'So you want a cup of tea or a beer? Or something?'

'No, Mr Carter, not now, thank you. We want to ask you about Daniel Winter. You're friends with him, yes?'

'Yeah, I guess. He's a mate. What of it?'

'His mother has reported him missing. Do you have any idea where he might be?'

'I saw him last night. We were in the park having a few beers.'

'What time last night?'

'About ten, I think. We stayed till at around midnight.'

'So you where with him until midnight, yes?'

'Yeah, more or less. Can't remember exactly. I was a bit pissed. You know what I mean.' This brings a smile to his face showing brown stained teeth.

'And you came back here, did you?'

'Yeah, I did.'

'Which way did Daniel go, do you remember?'

'He didn't. He was talking to some blokes by the swings. I told you I was a bit pissed, so I went home.'

'Which 'blokes' Mr Carter? This is really important. Can you describe them?'

'It was dark and they had their backs to me. I couldn't see their faces.'

'Anything, Mr Carter, anything at all will be a great help. What about the clothes they were wearing?'

'I said it was dark, and they were under the trees with their backs to me. I do remember seeing a van.'

'What kind of van? Think hard, Mr Carter. Please try.'

'Well, as I keep saying it was dark, you know it was midnight. But I think the van was black, and it could have been a VW of some sort. Yes, I'm sure now, it was a black VW van.'

CHAPTER NINETEEN

As Shand and Walker are driving back to the police station they are both deep in thought. Walker is looking out of the side window his hand stroking is chin. He turns to Shand.

'I don't understand, Sir. How can it be the same people?'

'I'm with you Robert. It doesn't add up. We have three dead bodies and three statues of the wise monkeys. But we're missing something. I just can't figure it out what. We have to dig deeper.'

Daniel Winter wakes to find himself in what he can only make out as a very big cave; he can hear the sea and smell the salt air, he looks down and sees leg irons cutting into his ankles that keep him chained to the rocks. He cannot remember how he got here. He has a taste of something in his throat, which he can't recognise. He feels extremely groggy. He looks around to sees an opening in the rocks, far in the distance where he can see the sun and clouds. He is confused, frightened and very cold.

Shand and Walker are back in their office. Walker is pacing around the room.

'I still don't get it, Sir. If it is the same people, why have they taken Daniel Winter? I've run his name through the computer. He's clean and not known to us.'

'I'm really worried, Robert. The way I see it is either they have taken the wrong man or they are beginning to enjoy a little too much what they are doing.'

'How do you mean, Sir? How can anyone 'enjoy this sort of thing?'

'Well, they hide behind some sort of peculiar ceremony to justify their killings. We now know they dress in blood red robes. We got that from Miss Collins. The last three victims were well known to us, nasty people, but none the less they didn't deserve that kind of horrific death.'

'Do you really think theses people, who ever they are, will just take anybody just so that they can conduct their weird ceremony?'

'I wish I knew, Sergeant, but for now we have to concentrate on finding our missing person.'

'Sir, Tom Carter mentioned a black van, a VW black van. Doesn't our local butcher Arthur Ambrose have a black van?'

'Yes he does, Sergeant. But it's not a VW. It's a Ford.'

'Maybe Carter got it wrong. It's worth a look, don't you think?'

'Okay, Sergeant, run with it. Let me know what you find?'

The Freohr meet in the usual place, Ebrithil is standing.

'Brethren, we have a new candidate who is being held in the smugglers' cave where we kept the last one. But we must wait for a few days before we deal with him. The police are still very active in their investigations. We don't want to make them suspicious about any of us.'

Frank de Caux stands up.

'Master, what has this candidate done to warrant our attention?'

Ebrithil gets up.

' He has been found guilty of rape, violent assault of the elderly, burglary and dealing drugs. He has evaded the police by never having been convicted because they cannot find anyone who will give evidence against him; they always say they didn't know who it was. He terrifies his victims into silence telling them if they spoke to the police he would find them and kill them. But we know he is guilty. We have evidence from one of his victims who talked to us. We promised her she would stay anonymous.'

Clancy Belet stands up.

'Master, how long can we keep him in the smugglers' cave before we perform the ceremony?'

'Time is on our side, brother. The police are concentrating all their efforts on the Castle grounds. That is unfortunate for us; we can't use that venue again. But we have many others at out disposal.

The smugglers' cave being one of the best we have with the secret passageways. We can come and go without anyone seeing us or being suspicious.'

The Freohr sit in silence until Ebrithil stands up again.

'Brethren are we finished here?'

No one says a word.

'All right, then. Make sure someone visits the candidate at least once a day. Just give him water, nothing else. When we perform the ceremony we don't want him resisting too much.'

CHAPTER TWENTY

Annabel is standing on the station platform waiting for Molly to arrive, when her mobile phone rings, the number withheld.

'Miss Christi?'

'Yes, how can I help?'

'You should be aware. The missing person Daniel Winter is guilty of numerous different crimes. He will be dealt with soon.'

The phone goes dead. Annabel looks at the screen hoping to see a number but sees nothing. She calls Neal immediately.

'Hi Annabel. Has Molly arrived yet?'

'No, not yet. Listen I've just had a weird phone call. I don't know who from the number was withheld just like last time.'

'Weird in what way?'

'He said the missing person Daniel Winter is guilty of numerous different crimes and he will be dealt with soon. Then he hung up.'

'Holy shit. You're kidding me. Please say you are, Annabel?'

'No Neal, I've never been more serious in my life.'

There is a long pause. Annabel can hear Neal breathing.

'Okay, leave it with me. Take Molly home, please. I'll see you both later.'

Shand immediately sets out to go and see the Chief. As he is walking along the corridor to his office he thinks to himself: 'how can I explain this?' He knocks on the door and a deep loud voice coming from inside tells Shand to enter.

'Morning, Sir. I have some bad news.'

'Come and sit down, Mr Shand. Tell me what have you got?'

'There's been a phone call, Sir. Miss Christi from the Local Newspaper received a call ten minutes ago. She immediately called me afterwards.'

'Who was the call from?'

'She doesn't know, Sir. The number was withheld.'

'Then tell me what did the person say, Mr Shand?'

'He said that Daniel Winter is guilty of numerous different crimes and will be dealt with soon. Then the phone went dead, Sir.'

The Chief is standing by the window looking out with his hands behind his back, turning them nervously as if he is drying them. Shand sees this and makes a mental note.

'Are you telling me, Mr Shand, that these people, who ever

they are, are now so confident that they are giving us warnings? And why is there another victim? I thought we had three already?'

'Yes, Sir. I'm puzzled as well. I have Sergeant Walker working on the history of the three wise monkeys to see what he can find. It doesn't make sense that they have taken a fourth person.'

The Chief turns and looks at Shand with glaring eyes. There are beads of sweat on his forehead. He sits at his desk placing his hands in his favourite position, as if in prayer.

'Tell me. What do you propose to do with this news, Mr Shand?'

'As I said, Sir, we are exploring all avenues possible.'

'Very well. I don't like this, Mr Shand. I don't like this at all. Find this person alive if possible. And soon. Do you understand?'

'We are doing our best, Sir. I'll keep you updated.'

'Very well.'

The Chief opens a folder on his desk and puts on his half moon glasses. This tells Shand the meeting is over. He walks to the door. The Chief continues looking at his paper work but says:

'Three dead bodies are three too many. We don't want a fourth do we, Mr Shand?'

Shand holding the door handle looks at the Chief with a irritated expression.

As he enters his office, Sergeant Walker is at his desk on the computer. Shand walks over and looks over his shoulder at the screen. Pictures of the three wise monkeys stare back at him.

'Have you found anything, Robert?'

'Yes, Sir. I have. And it's not good.'

'Great. All I need is more bad news this morning. Tell me what have you found?'

'I don't know why I didn't see this before, Sir. But according to history there was a fourth monkey. It was done away with, so to speak, in the 14th century. But none the less it was there for a long time.'

'Jesus, Robert, what are you telling me? What position did this monkey have?'

'According to this website, Sir, it was 'Feel no evil.' It had its hands over its heart. I already have its original name'

'Tell me Robert?'

'*Shizaru.*'

Shand drops into his chair staring at Sergeant Walker not saying a word. He cannot believe what he has just heard. He leans forward with his elbows on his desk, clasping his face in his hands trying to shut out everything hoping it will all go away. He looks up slowly gazing around his office trying to make some sense of it all. Then looks back at Sergeant Walker.

'We're right back where we started. We haven't got a clue who is doing this. Only now we know there's going to be a fourth murder and we aren't able to stop it. What I don't understand is why Annabel was given a warning'

'I don't know, Sir. But I need to see her and take her mobile. Maybe the lab can find something. I know they weren't successful last time but it's still worth a shot.'

'I agree, Robert. I've asked her to come to the station and give it to me. She should be here any minute. The desk Sergeant will bring her up.'

Shand walks to the coffee machine, lifts the jug to his cup, his hands shaking again. Walker seeing this, takes the coffee jug from him.

'Allow me, Sir.'

Sergeant Manning knocks on the door and puts his head around it.

'Sir. Miss Christi to see you.'

'Thanks, Bob. Show her in please.'

Annabel walks in looking as stunning as ever. She is wearing a two-piece suit in an emerald green, which complements her eyes and her vermillion coloured flowing hair. Brown high-heeled shoes complete her fabulous ensemble. Both Shand and Walker take a deep breath.

'Morning, you two. Robert, here's my phone. How long will you need it for?'

'Morning, Miss Christi. I'm not sure I'll take it to the lab now and let you know later if they find anything.'

Walker leaves the office. Neal and Annabel are alone; she looks at him with anxiety in her eyes as she sits at his desk.

'You look terrible, Neal.'

'It's going from worse to exceptionally worse. And that's an understatement. These people are now announcing their next murder and there's nothing I can do to stop it. I have absolutely no idea who's doing this. Sergeant Walker discovered this morning that there was a fourth wise monkey. So we can assume the missing person and the warning on your phone are connected, so we can expect a dead body any day now'

CHAPTER TWENTY-ONE

Sergeant Walker is with the forensic team in the lab, they are looking at Annabel's phone. They have all kinds of new technology at their disposal to help them. One of the forensic team has it connected to his computer. He is looking intently at the screen, his fingers tapping at the keyboard faster than a professional secretary.

'I think I have something here, Sergeant?'

He walks to the desk where the police forensic scientist is working.

'What have you got?'

'Let me try something else before, to be in no doubt.'

The scientist is busy tapping more keys on his keyboard. The screen on his computer is scrolling down so fast Walker has to look away.

'Bingo. There you are, Sergeant.'

Walker looks over the scientist's shoulder. He cannot believe what he sees. A mobile phone number is staring back at him glowing on the computer screen. He grabs his phone and dials Shand.

'Sir, we have a number. I'll get the details and be with you shortly.'

Shand puts his phone down and looks at Annabel. His face is perky.

'Who was that, Neal?'

'Sergeant Walker from the lab. They have traced a number from your phone. Let's hope it's not your mothers.'

Walker comes bursting into the office with a sheet of paper in is hand.

'I have it, Sir. They can even say where the chip was bought.'

'Show me, Sergeant.'

Shand takes the paper from Walker and holds it delicately as if it were a newborn baby. He turns it over in his hands looking at each and every word, scrutinising each letter making sure he does not miss a thing.

'At last, something positive. Get the car ready, Robert, we're going shopping.'

Annabel looks at Neal. He can tell what she is about to say.

'Yes, Annabel, you can come as well.'

An unmarked car with a driver is waiting for the three of them as they walk out side. The Chief joins them.

'The lab called me with their find, Mr Shand. May I ask, where are you off to?'

'We have a number, and the name of the shop where the chip was sold, Sir. We're going there now, hopefully to get the name of the person who purchased it.'

'Very well, Mr Shand. I'll be waiting for your report.'

As they drive away from the police station Shand looks through the back window where he can see the Chief still standing there with his hands behind his back, no doubt turning them over and over.

They pull up outside the shop where the chip was purchased. There is a sign on the door so Walker gets out of the car and walks over to get a better look. He turns around and walks back to the car. Shand opens his window.

'What does the sign say, Robert?'

'Closed, Sir. It's Thursday, half day closing.'

Shand drops heavily back in his seat. Annabel looks at him with real concern on her face, and then she turns to Robert.

'Doesn't it say where the owner can be found?'

'Nothing on the door. We'll have to get the police station to find the owner. It will take a while. I'll call it in now.'

Shand and Annabel get out of the car and stand on the pavement. Walker is in the car with the driver on the radio.

'If I were a smoker I think I would be on my third packet by now.'

Annabel smiles.

'Probably your fourth, and I think I would have joined you.'

Walker gets out of the car walks over to them.

'We've found him, Sir. His name is Mr Trevelling. He's on his way. He didn't sound too happy being called out on his half day off.'

'I don't give a shit, Sergeant. This is more important than any half a day off.'

The time seems to drag on slowly. All three of them are pacing backwards and forwards and in front of the shop looking up and down the street for the owner to appear. Shand looks over at the police car where the driver is asleep, his chin resting on his chest moving slowly up and down with each breath.

Eventually a man appears walking with determination towards the shop with a set of keys in is hand. Shand stands up straight to give him authority over this man. He looks at Shand then to Annabel and Walker.

'Are you the ones who called me out on my half day off?'

'I'm Detective Chief Inspector Shand and this is Detective Sergeant Walker. They both show their warrant cards. Miss Christi is here as an observer from the press. It is vitally important that we speak to you about a pre-paid chip that was sold from your shop.'

'Well, if you must. I suppose you had better come in.'

Shand shows the shopkeeper the print out of the mobile number.

'We have traced it to this shop and we need you to tell us who bought this number?'

The shopkeeper looks at Shand and Walker, and to the number. He has a cursory glance at Annabel smilling at her. He then looks up at all three of them.

'I'm sorry, I can't do that. It's confidential information. You must know this.'

All three of them look at each other in disbelief. Shand turns back to Mr Trevelling.

'Are you telling me you can't, or won't give me the details?'

'I can't, it's private information. I'm not able to just hand out this kind of thing to anyone who walks into my shop. You, of all people, must understand this.'

'First of all, Mr Trevelling we are not just 'anyone.' We are the police, and we are also investigation a triple murder enquiry. You have no doubt read about it in the news papers.'

'Yes, of course, I have. Who hasn't? But the fact remains I can't give you this information. It's private and confidential.'

'Then you leave me with no choice Mr Trevelling. I'm arresting you for obstruction of a police officer in the course of his duty.'

Shand turns to Walker.

'Take him to the car, Sergeant. We will finish this at the police station. Bring all this information with you, Mr Trevelling. I'm going to need it.'

Trevelling is standing there not believing what he has just heard. He stares at all three of them hoping for some kind of help.

'Hold on just a minute. You can't arrest me for this, can you?' he asks with a look of disbelief in his eyes.

Shand goes to stand in front of him looking down. He has the advantage of height, which gives him an authoritarian posture.

'I told you, Mr Trevelling this is a murder investigation. You are holding evidence that could lead us to the people concerned. I'm not prepared to stand here and argue with you about this, one way or another I'm going to get the information I need. It's up to you. We can do this here or at the police station. You choose.'

'Okay. Okay here you are, take it. I just hope I won't get into trouble over this.'

'Thank you, Mr Trevelling. You have been most helpful. I won't forget it.'

They all three turn and walk out of the shop, across the street to the car. Shand opens the door for Annabel. The slam of the doors awakens the driver with a jump.

'The police station, quick as possible.'

Shand looks at the paper Trevelling gave him. His eyes open wide at what he is reading. Annabel sees this.

'What is it, Neal?'

Walker looks round from the front seat first at Annabel then at Shand.

'Does it give a name, Sir?'

'Yes, Robert, it does. And you're never going to believe who's.'

CHAPTER TWENTY-TWO

The Celtic Knot is very busy for a Thursday night. Harvey Ventura has to work behind the bar because his barmaid Jenny called in sick with the flu. He has better things to do but it will have to wait. He sees Clancy Belet and Frank de Caux sitting at a table drinking and talking to each other. He walks over to collect glasses.

'I don't often see you two in here on a Thursday night.'

They both look at him with contempt in their eyes.

'As you're not free we have had to postpone our gathering, haven't we?'

'It's not my fault. I cant just close the pub can I?' People would ask questions.'

'I guess. But you know who's not very happy about this, don't you?'

'Yes, I know. I called him earlier to explain. He understands. We'll have our amusement soon. Don't worry. Drink up, the next one is on the house.'

Suddenly the door opens and Arthur Ambrose walks in. Ventura points to the table where his colleagues are sitting.

'Go and join them. I'll bring you a drink.'

He goes to sit with the others.

'Evening lads. How are we this evening? Having fun?'

They look at him with disgust.

'You find this funny, do you?'

Ambrose shrugs his shoulders.

'Not really no, but what else can we do?'

Clancy Belet, turns to him, opens his mouth to speak, but Frank de Caux stops him with a wave of his hand.

'Not here, not now. You know the rules.'

Clancy Belet finishes his drink, slams his glass down on the table and storms out of the pub. The rest stay at their table looking at each other. Harvey Ventura walks over to their table.

'What was that all about?'

Frank de Caux looks at Ventura.

'He's a bit wound up. Take no notice. I'll talk to him.'

'Make sure you do, we don't want any loose cannons do we? Or we might have to deal with him ourselves, there's too much at stake to fuck it all up now, I'll have to have a word with the Worshipful Master.'

'There's no need for that. I said I'd speak to him, okay?'

'No, it's not okay?' Ventura leans across the table and whispers in Frank de Caux's ear. He is so close to de Caux that he can smell his tobacco breath. 'I'm not going to spend the rest of my life in some stinking, fucking prison cell because that little prick can't handle the work anymore, understand? 'Now get out of my pub and see to him before he fucks everything up.'

Neal Shand is still in some kind of shock from the information he discovered from the mobile phone shop. He sits at his desk starring at the piece of paper in his hands. Sergeant Walker is at his desk. Swiftly he spins round in his chair and looks at Shand.

'Aren't you going to share this information with me, Sir?'

'Not for the moment, Robert. You'll have to trust me with it for a while longer. There's someone I have to talk to first.'

'Up to you, Sir, but if it's going to lead us to whoever is committing these murders I should really be told who's name is on that piece of paper your holding.'

Annabel is waiting on the platform for Molly's train to arrive. When her mobile
Rings, she jumps with fright until she sees Neal's name on the screen. All these calls from mysterious people have taken its toll on her.
'Hello sweetheart how are you?'
'Hello, hope you're feeling okay. Has Molly's train arrived yet?'
'I can see it now. She'll be here in two minutes. Shall I take her to your house?'
'Yes, please, and could you pick up a bottle of wine or two? I need a drink tonight.'
'Okay. How long will you be?'
'I just have to speak to someone and I'll be home straight afterwards.'

Shand's mind is racing. He is not sure what to do next. He stands up from his desk, walks over to the coffee machine, picks up his favourite mug and pours himself some coffee. His hands are perfectly still. Then he walks from his office to the stairs where he sees Sergeant Manning coming on duty.
'Evening, Sir. Still here?'
'It would seem so Bob. It's like I live here these days. Is the

Chief in his office?'

'Yes, Sir. But he has someone with him and asked not to be disturbed.'

'Who is with him Bob?'

'Doctor Cole, I think, Sir. I didn't get a good look but I think it's him.'

Shand rooted to the spot doesn't know whether to knock on the Chief's door or leave it till the morning. He keeps telling himself: 'I have to know. There is a person's life at risk.' In thought he slowly carries on up the stairs. He stops outside the Chief's door hand raised to knock. It is as if there is a force field between him and the Chief's door. He is paralysed. He closes his eyes and forces himself to bang on the door. The next thing he hears is the Chief's voice.

'Come.'

Shand pushes the door that feels like it is made of lead. As he enters the room he sees the Chief standing at the window, hands in their usual position behind his back.

'What can I do for you, Mr Shand? As you can see I have company.'

Shand looks around the very large office and sees someone sitting by a settee. He cannot make out whom it is because the evening sun is flooding through the window opposite him thus concealing the man's face.

'Sir, I have new evidence about the murder case.'

'Go on, Mr Shand, I'm all ears.'

The Chief doesn't bother to introduce his visitor to Shand.

'I have a name to the phone number we traced. The one who has been calling Miss Christi's mobile phone?'

The Chief turns to face Shand, still ignoring the person sitting on the settee.

'Interesting, Mr Shand. Leave it on my desk, would you? I'll see to it later.'

'But, Sir, this is the best lead we've had so far in this case. We have a name and you won't believe who it is.'

'I said, put it on my desk. There's a good fellow. I will see to it presently understood?'

Shand cannot understand why the Chief is being so relaxed about this; he moves closer to the desk and places the sheet of paper with the name and number on it, pushing it slowly to the middle. He looks up at the Chief who has turned back to look out of the window. He tries to look at the person sitting but he cannot see the face clearly. The Chief speaks without looking at Shand.

'Do nothing, Mr Shand, till I speak with you tomorrow. Understood? Now go home.'

'Yes, Sir, I understand. See you in the morning.'

Shand standing by his car, keys ready to unlock the door, his head spinning, tries to understand what he just experienced in the Chief's office. He also tries to figure out whom the person was sitting on that settee.

He starts his beloved beetle. The very characteristic noise of the car usually puts a smirk on his face, except this time he does not really notice it, he just drives away heading for home. As he parks outside his house, he can see the curtains moving. It is Molly watching for him. She opens the front door and comes running to him, arms open wide: She jumps on him hugging so hard he can hardly breath.

'Hi, Dad. How are you?'

He will never get used to these moments, they are much too special to him. He has to push her softly away to see her face so he can kiss her.

'I'm so much better for seeing you, darling. Did you have a good trip?'

'Yes, fine. Annabel met me at the station.'

'Lets go in, shall we? Is Annabel still here?'

'Yes, I told her she had to stay for dinner. And maybe the night! Molly looks at her father with a grin. 'She's brought Sherper as well so we can all go for a walk after dinner, can't we?'

'Anything you want, precious.'

As they enter the living room Annabel is waiting with a bottle of red wine and a cork screw, holding them out for Neal to take,

'Your job, I think, Detective.'

He moves between her arms and tenderly kisses both cheeks.

'Thank you. I need a drink.'

Even though Molly is in the house with him Annabel detects a vagueness about Neal. He seems distant, not really listening to Molly as she tells him about her exams. He sees Annabel looking at him with concern. He puts his finger to his mouth as if to say, not now. Not in front of Molly.

After dinner they all take Sherper for a walk. It's a beautiful, calm, and warm night. Molly runs ahead with Sherper. Neal and Annabel walk slowly behind. She puts her arm through his and kisses him on his cheek.

'What's wrong, Neal? I can see something is troubling you.'

They keep walking. Neal looks up at the sky and then to Annabel.

'Do you see those stars, Annabel?' Right now I wish I were up there with them twinkling away with nothing to worry about.'

'Tell me, Neal. You're beginning to frighten me.'

He stops and looks into Annabel's eyes. He pulls her close to him resting his chin on her shoulder letting out a sigh.

'You know the evidence I got from the mobile phone shop the other day?'

'Yes, you have a name connected to the number that called me. And you still won't tell me who it is, will you?'

'I can't, not yet. I had to talk to the Chief first.'

'You did that today, didn't you?'

'Yes, just before I left the police station.'

'And what did he say?'

'That's what's bothering me, Annabel, he didn't say anything. He told me to leave it with him, and that he will discuss it with me in the morning. And there's something else.'

'What?'

'There was someone else in his office sitting on the settee. Unfortunately I couldn't see who it was and the Chief never introduced us. It was very peculiar. The man just sat there not saying a word. He had his back to me. And the Chief acted as if there was no one else in the room.

'Just ask him next time you speak to him. It could be important to the case.'

'Yes. I will.'

They stand there holding each other closely listening to the waves crashing against the rocks when Molly comes running towards them with Sherper in hot pursuit shouting: 'Stop it, you two, not in front of the children.'

Several hundred feet below the cliffs, Daniel Winter is lying in the foetal position trying to keep warm; he still doesn't know why he is being held captive or by whom; all he knows is he is freezing, starving, and very wet. The heavy rusty chains holding him are beginning to cut into his ankle causing bleeding. Every time he moves to try and find a more comfortable position the chains cut deeper into his leg. He still cannot see anything apart from a small beam of light in the distance and which is slowly disappearing. This tells him it must be heading towards nightfall. He cannot remember how long he has been there. The two men that came earlier said nothing to him, they just left a small bottle of water. One of them kicked him in his face as hard as he could, making him hazy. The other one kicked him in the groin. This made him want to throw up, but he had nothing in his stomach, no food to bring up. He was just reaching coughing up bile.

He feels he had lost a tooth. With his lips swollen he finds it hard to drink from the bottle. He tries to shout out again for help but the sound of the waves being far too noisy cover all his efforts. He starts to cry again. He has never felt so frightened and lonely in his life.

CHAPTER TWENTY-THREE

The Chief Constable is clearing his desk when his visitor stands up to look at him.

'This Mr Shand?'

The Chief turns to look at his guest.

'Yes, what about him?'

'He's very meticulous in is work. It could be a problem, don't you think?'

'DCI Shand is one of my best policemen that's why I put him in charge of this case. Does it worry you?'

'Quite frankly, yes, it does. He's going to keep investigating till he finds out who is behind these murders.'

'That's his job. I don't see it being a problem though, if you and your colleagues keep to the procedures we agreed to.

The visitor leaves without saying another word making sure

he uses the back door reserved only for the Chief Constable and his staff.

The duty sergeant standing by the back door smoking a cigarette sees a figure walking away with purpose. The sergeant thinks he recognises the person but can't be sure. He can only see the back of him as he vanishes into the darkness. Just has he is stubbing out his cigarette the Chief appears heading for his car. Sergeant Manning calls out:

'Good night, Sir.' But he gets no reply.

The Chief seems very preoccupied. Sergeant Manning shrugs his shoulders and walks back inside the police station.

Shand is up early having had a restless night; he is in the kitchen making coffee as Annabel walks in. He turns to look at her, even first thing in the morning she looks astonishing.

'Morning, Gorgeous, coffee?'

'Hmm, yes please. You're up early. You were tossing and turning all night.'

'Sorry about that. It's this business with the Chief last night. I can't stop thinking about it. He was very peculiar in his approach towards me. I'm going to confront him first thing this morning as soon as I get to the Police station.'

'Good. You need to get to the end of this. It's not normal someone like him should be so elusive about something so serious.'

Molly walks into the kitchen with a towel around her head

and wearing a bathrobe. She takes Neal's cup from his hand and drinks from it.

'Thanks, Dad. What's for breakfast?'

The drive to the police station seemed to take no time as Shand was thinking about what he was gong to say to the Chief. As he parks his Beetle in his place he can see the Chief's car is already there. He has his speech ready having gone over and over it on the way in his car. Walking to the front entrance he sees sergeant Manning heading towards him.

'Morning, Bob. A peaceful night I hope?'

'Yes, nothing to tell you. Just a couple of drunks causing trouble in the Celtic Knot. They're sleeping it off in the cells. Tell me, Sir. Did the Chief have a visitor last night?'

'Why do you ask, Bob?'

'Well, I was standing by the back door having a cigarette, when all of a sudden someone came out of the Chief's back door and walked off quite fast. Closely followed by the Chief who ignored me when I said goodnight.'

'Did you see who it was?'

'Sorry, no, it was getting dark and I didn't have my glasses on. I only saw a silhouette of a man walking away. But I did think he looked familiar in the way he was walking.'

'Who do you think it was Bob? It's very important. I saw someone in the Chief's office last night but we weren't introduced. He was sitting on the Chief's settee. I couldn't see him clearly as he had his back to me. It's a big office and the light was bad.'

'Well, Sir, it's just a guess, and I can't be sure, but it looked like Doctor Cole. I'll have to have a word with the Chief. All guests have to be lodged in the visitors' book.'

Shand is staring at sergeant Manning his mouth opening but nothing coming from it he thinks: 'Why would Doctor Cole be in the Chief's office and more significantly why didn't the Chief introduce him if it was him? What is he hiding?'

'Are you all right, Sir? You look like you've seen a ghost.'

'I'm fine, Bob. Please don't say anything about this till I speak to the Chief okay?'

'Okay, Sir. But we can't have people coming and going as they wish. This is a police station. Anyway I'll leave it with you, see you later.'

Shand, once again, finds himself outside the Chief's office with his hand raised to knock on the door, but there seems to be a force field stopping him. He takes a deep breath closes his eyes and knocks hard twice on the door.

'Come,' is all he can hear. The door seems to open sluggishly and clumsily as if it was made of lead. He walks to the front of the Chief's desk, which seems like it has swelled in size since last night.

'Mr Shand, what can I do for you?'

'Sir, it's about the name I gave you, and I need to know who was here with you last night.'

'Concerning the name, I'm looking into it. And as for my guest all I can say, it was a fellow lodge member. Do you understand me? I can't and won't disclose his identity to you, or anyone.'

The Chief is glaring at Shand with eyes that say: 'don't ask anymore questions'

'Very well, Sir. But I need to know what you want me to do with this new evidence we have regarding the name connected to the mobile phone, that was used to call Miss Christi warning her off talking to us.'

'I understand your impatience, Mr Shand. I think because of whom it is I should take it from here and speak to him myself. I'm going to do it this morning. Leave it with me, will you? When I get back I will come and find you. Anything else Mr Shand? I'm busy, and so are you.'

'No, Sir. I'll look forward to our meeting later.'

Shand walks back to his office with fuzziness in his head thinking that none of this makes any sense to him. A Chief Constable should not be pulling rank and taking away his investigation.

He sees Sergeant Walker at his desk.

'Morning, Sir. Good meeting with the Chief? Are you going to tell me the name now?'

'Morning, Robert. No not really. I need you to do something important for me but it's a bit unusual.'

'Go on, Sir, tell me.'

'Keep this to yourself and talk to no one but me, okay?'

'Understood, Sir.'

'I want you to follow the Chief this morning, and for God's sake don't let him see you.'

Walker stands up, closes the door behind Shand.

'Sir, tell me again, I don't think I completely understood what you just said.'

'I know it sounds strange, Robert, but I need to know who he is going to see this morning.'

'Why don't you just ask him?'

'I just did. He's being very evasive, and I don't want to wait until he thinks it's time I should know. This is the first major break we've had in this investigation, Robert. And for some reason the Chief has taken it onto himself to take over. Plus he's dragging his heels with it. I don't like this, Robert. If I have to go over his head I will but first I need to know who he is seeing this morning.'

'Very well, Sir. I'll do my best.'

'Remember, Robert, speak to no one but me. Call me as soon as you have anything, understood?'

Shand pours a coffee and sits at his desk trying to figure out what is happening to him; he can't understand all the obstacles he keeps coming up against. Three of the most sickening murders in history, and he has only one clue, a name.

Molly and Annabel are becoming very close. They like a lot of the same things despite their difference in age. The same music, art and fashions. They are spending the day together shopping and having lunch. The town is hectic. There are lots of tourists this time of year. They find it hard to get a table in Molly's favourite restaurant. They wait at the bar having a glass of wine. Annabel looks round to see if a table has become free. The waiters are franticly running backwards and forwards from the kitchen. She sees two people at a table in the corner of the restaurant.

'That's funny.'

Molly looks at her with inquisitiveness.

'What's funny Annabel?'

'Over there in the corner. I'm sure that's the Chief Constable. But I can't see who he's with.'

Molly stands up and tries to see more clearly.

'No I can't make him out either. But you know even Chief Constables have to eat too, Annabel. It's not that unusual to see him here. It's a very popular restaurant.'

'No. I guess not. It's just I know Neal had a meeting with him this morning. I wonder how that went.'

What they both failed to see was Sergeant Walker outside in an unmarked car taking photos of the restaurant.

CHAPTER TWENTY-FOUR

Daniel Winter is woken by a powerful kick to his stomach. He sees two men standing over him. One of them has a bottle of water in his hand.

'Breakfast, you did call for room service didn't you?'

they both laugh loudly while looking down at their prisoner.

He puts the bottle of water down beside him. Then both of the Frehor go and stand over him looking intensely into his eyes.

'What do you want? Why are you keeping me here? I've done nothing wrong.'

'Oh, but you have, haven't you? Numerous heinous crimes. But you have always got away with it until now. We know what you've been up to, and who you raped, and molested and then terrified them into silence. It sickens us to look at you.'

'But why are you keeping me here? Take me to the police, you can't treat me like this it's not human.'
They both look at him and laugh out loud again. One of them leans close to his face.

'You're not a fucking human. And we're here to make sure you get what you deserve.'

The force of the punch to his face sends him reeling back on the rocks banging his head, making him hazy, his face turning ashen white. The chain on his ankle cuts deeper as he falls. He cries out in pain. The two Freohr stand there looking and grinning at each other, knowing their time will come soon to perform the ceremony that they have started to enjoy too much on their victim.

'Don't you go running off and tell your mummy on us.'

The two Freohr turn and walk away still laughing out loud slapping each other on the back. Daniel Winter cries out to them.

'Wait, please, don't leave me here.'

One of the Freohr turns to look at him.

'Why, are you lonely?'

Throwing his head back in raptures of joy.

Daniel Winter lying on the wet jagged rocks clutches to his chest the bottle of water muttering repeatedly under his breath.

'Please help. For Gods sake someone please help me.'

He watches the two Freohr disappear into the distance, leaving him alone, desolate and petrified.

Annabel and Molly eventually get a table. As they are looking through the menu Annabel cannot help looking over to the corner table where she thinks the Chief Constable is sitting with someone, who she still cannot quite see properly because there is a large bamboo plant which divides the dining area into two rooms obscuring her vision.

'It all looks so wonderful, doesn't it, Annabel? I don't know what to choose.'

'Yes. Molly, will you pick something for me? I'm just going to the ladies room.'

She purposely walks towards the corner table on her way to the toilet. She can now see who the Chief is having lunch with. Just as she is passing he looks straight at her. She cannot avoid his glare.

'Good day, Miss Christi. I didn't know you frequented this restaurant?

'Hello. This is my first time here. And you? Are you enjoying your lunch?'

'Yes, thank you. Let me introduce you to my guest. He

waves his hand across the table. A man of prominence stands up extending his hand out open to clasp hers. He is tall, handsome, and has a look of distinction about him. He is wearing an exquisitely cut suit with a gleaming white shirt and complementary grey silk tie. He looks straight into her eyes making her feel uncomfortable as if he is mentally undressing her; she holds her hand out to greet him.

'Good day Miss Christi. My name is. James Brodie. I'm very pleased to meet you. Will you join us?'

He has her hand in his, holding it with a very firm grip.

'Thank you for the invitation, but I'm with a friend.'

'A pity, maybe another time.'

Still holding onto her hand softly, he caresses it. She feels as if he is trying to abduct her. This makes her quite anxious.

She pulls her hand from his.

'As I said, I'm with a friend.'

He says nothing, just stares at her with probing eyes, smiling as he sits down.

Annabel walks back to her table. Molly looks up at her.

'Are you okay? You look a bit flushed.'

'I'm fine. What did you order for me?'

Outside sergeant Walker is patiently waiting in his car with his camera. His mobile phone rings.

'Hello. DS Walker.'

'Robert, it's Shand. Where are you?'

'I'm outside the Riverview restaurant, Sir. The Chief has

been inside for over an hour. He's with someone but I still can't see whom. As soon as they leave I'll get a photo for you. Oh, and your daughter is in there as well with Miss Christi from the local Gazette.'

'I know about them. It's the Chief I'm more interested in and who he's with.'

'Do I stay here, Sir? Or come back to the station.'

'Stay there, Robert. I really would like to know who's so important that the Chief can take a long leisurely lunch, instead of finding out who this mobile number belongs to.'

Shand hangs up and heads for the coffee machine for the hundredth time this morning or so it seems. As he is pouring, his mobile rings. It is Annabel.

'Hello, sexy. Are you having fun with my daughter?'

'Hi. Yes we're having lunch at the Riverview Restaurant. And guess who's here as well?'

'Enlighten me. I'm not very good at guessing.'

'Your illustrious Chief Constable, and a friend. I was just introduced to him.'

Shand sits up in his chair looking for a pen to write with.

'That's very interesting. Did you get a name?'

'Yes of course. His name is. James Brodie. Have you ever heard of him?'

'Well, if it's the same Sir James Brodie who's a high court judge, then yes I have.'

Sergeant Walker is watching as the Chief and James Brodie walk from the restaurant and stand on the pavement talking. This is a perfect opportunity for taking photos. After a minute they both go their different ways. Walker packs away his camera and heads back to the police station.

A knock on his office door wakens Shand from his thoughts. He sees the Chief put his head round the door.

'My office, please, Mr Shand.' He then disappears.

Just as he is about to leave sergeant Walker comes in clutching his digital camera.

'Sir, take a look at these.'

'I'm sorry, Robert. I've just been summonsed upstairs. But I know whom he had lunch with. Thanks anyway for your efforts, we'll speak later.'

As Shand enters the office, he sees the Chief in his usual place by the window arms behind him, hands clasping.

'Sit down, Mr Shand.'

The Chief turns to look at him smiling.

'So, Mr Shand, I suppose you're wondering why I've taken so long to respond to your request about the name, aren't you?'

'To be perfectly honest, Sir, yes I am.'

'I've just had lunch with Sir James Brodie. You know who he is I assume?'

'Yes, Sir, I've heard of him. A very influential man.'

'Yes, indeed. Well, I needed to talk with him before I took any action about the name we have. You see, Mr Shand, the person implicated is also a very important person in the community. We

155

can't go and arrest him just because his name appears in connection with a mobile phone number. Do you see what I'm getting at?'

'Yes, Sir. But the fact remains his name is connected, and I find that very disturbing considering who he is.'

'I understand. Now, Sir James has advised me to do nothing at this time.'

Shand stands up looking straight at the Chief with a look of ambiguity on his face.

'Sir, with all due respect, we cannot just ignore this piece of evidence, it's all we have to go on. And not overlooking the fact we have another missing person. We need to interview this individual to find out why his name came up on the records. He may be able to lead us to Daniel Winter. Time is not on our side. He's been missing for four days and we still haven't got a clue where he could be'

'Mr Shand, that's an order. Do nothing with this evidence until I say otherwise.'

Shand cannot believe what he is hearing.

The Chief is standing leaning across his desk glaring into his eyes.

'I want you to concentrate on finding our missing person. Put all your efforts into that and nothing else. Do I make myself clear?'

'Crystal clear, Sir. But I want you to know for the record I do not agree with you or Sir James. I can't help feeling you're withholding vital evidence.'

He turns and storms out of the office before the Chief can respond slamming the door so hard the walls shudder.

Back in his office he paces up and down like an expectant father, one hand on his forehead. He feels as if his brain was going to explode at any minute. Sergeant Walker seeing this comes to him with a mug of coffee. Shand takes it thanking him. He takes a sip nearly spiting it back up.

'Jesus, Robert, what have you put in this? It tastes like fire water.'

'Just a different kind of 'milk', Sir. I thought you could do with a soother after your meeting with the Chief, which I'm guessing didn't go very well judging by the way you nearly pulled his door off its hinges.'

'Thanks, Robert. Yes you're right it didn't go well at all. In fact I'm really concerned about his reaction to all this. I'm not sure where to go next. He told me to concentrate on finding our missing person and do nothing with the name I have until he tells me otherwise.'

'So, what are you going to do?'

'I'm going to ask for a meeting with the Minister. I don't care if the Chief doesn't like it. Daniel Winter is out there somewhere and we have to find him before it's too late, I don't want any more murders on my turf. Understand, Robert?'

'Completely, Sir. I'm with you all the way on this, you can trust me.'

'Thanks, Robert, I can use a friend and colleague right now. Someone I can rely on.'

CHAPTER TWENTY-FIVE

Arranging a meeting with a cabinet minister is never an easy task. Following numerous phone calls to various secretaries and assistants Shand got his man on the phone. Lord Huxley was at first reluctant to speak, but Shand persisted and would not take 'no' for an answer. After several minutes explaining, Lord Huxley said.

'Mr Shand, I don't think we can do much over the phone. Can you come to see me?'

'Yes, Sir, but I'm afraid time is not on my side. Daniel Winter has been missing for almost five days now. I'm extremely worried it might be too late if I loose time coming up to London.'

'I understand. I'm going to call the Chief and tell him you're going to act on the name you have. If you get any fallout from it, call me back and I'll smooth things over with him. Don't forget now I'm involved you must keep me updated of everything that happens. Do you follow?'

'Yes, Sir, fully. Thank you for helping. I don't think the Chief is going to be very pleased when he hears what I've done, but I had no choice.'

'Don't worry about the Chief, Mr Shand. Leave him to me. Put all your energies into finding this missing person.'

Shand puts the phone back into its cradle and looks over to Robert.

'Okay, Sergeant. We have a suspect to interview. Come with me.'

Driving into town Sergeant Walker can't resist asking:

'Where are we going, Sir?'

'To see a Doctor, Sergeant.'

'Are you not feeling well, Sir?'

'On the contrary, Robert, I'm feeling better than I have for days.'

At the surgery Shand and Walker are in the waiting room having been told the Doctor has a patient with him. Walker turns to Shand.

'Are you sure it was the doctor's name connected with the mobile phone?'

'Yes, Sergeant, very sure. I've checked a dozen times and I'm in no doubt it's his name. My only concern is he's going to deny all knowledge.'

'We have it in writing, Sir. Official records from the phone company. How can he deny it?'

'That's what we are going to find out any minute I hope.'

The door opens and Doctor Cole puts his head round looking for his next patient. He looks confused when he sees the two policemen sitting there.

'Mr Shand, Sergeant Walker, what can I do for you?'

'I think we had better go into your surgery Doctor. We need to talk to you. It's very important.'

'Very well. Follow me please.'

'Okay, I'm all yours gentlemen. Tell me what is this all about?'

'Your name has been connected with a mobile phone number that was used twice to warn Miss Christi from talking about the body she found on the beach. Do you recognise this number?

' Shand shows a piece of paper with the number on it.

Doctor Cole takes it, repeating the number to himself. He looks back at Shand and Walker in turn.

'I'm sorry, gentlemen, I don't know this number, it means nothing to me I'm afraid.'

He hands back the sheet of paper to Shand.

'Tell me then, Doctor, why did your name come up as the regiestered owner of this number?'

'I've really no idea. It must be a mistake of some sort. Now if you don't mind I have patients to see. Good day to you both.'

Shand puts the piece of paper in his pocket looking at Doctor Cole who's looking back unpleasantly at him.

'I'm sorry, Doctor, I'm not satisfied with your answer. I think you had better come with us to the police station for a formal interview.'

'What? Are you serious? Are you arresting me?'

'If I have to, Doctor, then, yes, I'm arresting you on suspicion of withholding evidence in a murder enquiry. Caution him, will you, Sergeant?'

Doctor Cole looks at Shand not knowing what to say next. He starts to tremble and small beads of perspiration form on his forehead.

'This is an outrage. You know I'm closely connected with the Chief Constable. Don't you? I'll have your job for this, Chief Inspector. You see if I don't.'

'That's Detective Chief Inspector to you, Doctor Cole. And I would advise you to say nothing more until we're in the interview room at the police station.'

The interview room is an gloomy and featureless place. There is one-table with four chairs, a fixed tape recorder placed on the table. There are no windows, just one light fixed to the ceiling. Doctor Cole with his solicitor sits opposite Shand and Walker. Shand leans forward pushing the red record button on the tape recorder.

'I'm Detective Chief Inspector Shand. Also present is Detective Sergeant Walker. The two other persons in the room are?' He gestures for them to speak. They both say their names.

'Today is Friday the twenty first of September. The time is four thirty pm. Doctor Cole, I asked you in your surgery about a mobile phone number which you deny having any knowledge of. Is that correct?'

Cole just nods his head in agreement looking at his solicitor for some sort of encouragement.

'I need you to say the words for the tape, Doctor. Now please try again?'

'No, I have never seen this number before. It's nothing to do with me.'

'Then how do you explain your name appearing on the phone company records when we traced it? You are the registered owner of this mobile phone number. This is the same number used to frighten off a witness to a murder inquiry, and maybe subsequent murders since.'

'I told you I don't know. Can I go now?'

Doctor Cole is very agitated and tense. He keeps looking at his solicitor who remains silent whilst writing on his legal pad, taking no notice of Doctor Cole's fretfulness.

'No, I'm afraid you can't go just yet, Doctor. I haven't had a truthful response to my questions. This evidence links you to at least one murder and you know there have been two more. You were the physician on call who performed the post mortems, weren't you?'

'Yes, you know I was, but I didn't kill anyone. I swear it.'

All of a sudden there is a firm knock at the door. Shand looks round to see the Chief standing there.

'For the benefit of the tape, Chief Constable Simmonds has just entered the room.'

He leans close to Shand's shoulder and in a whisper saying,

'May I have a word, please Mr Shand?'

Shand looks at his watch.

'Interview terminated at four fifty p.m. precisely.'

He leans forward and turns off the tape recorder.

'Sergeant Walker, take Doctor Cole to a holding cell please. We will need to interview him further.'

Doctor Cole stares at the Chief Constable in disbelieve with wide troubled eyes imploring him to help while he is being led away to the cells.

Upstairs in his office the Chief is remarkably composed sitting in his chair.

'Do you know who called me today, Mr Shand?'

'I would hazard a guess at Lord Huxley Sir.'

'And you would be right, Neal.'

This puts Shand a little off guard; the Chief has never used his first name before.

'The Minister and I had a long and very thought-provoking conversation. He put me in no doubt that I'm to give you all the support I can, regarding these murders.

'I'm glad to hear this, Sir. Maybe now I can go downstairs and re- interview Doctor Cole. I believe he's not being entirely honest with me.'

'You have my support. It's a shame it had to come to involving Lord Huxley. I don't like washing our dirty linen in public. I prefer to keep this in house, so to speak. Do you get my drift, Neal?'

'You were holding me back in my investigations, Sir. I had no choice but to go over your head. I will do it again if I have to. My main concern is to find the people responsible for these sickening murders. Not forgetting there could be one more as we're no closer to finding Daniel Winter. As far as I'm concerned I'm going to hold Doctor Cole for as long as it takes to get the truth from him. I can hold him for thirty-six hours now. And if I have to I will request another thirty-six if I think it's necessary.'

Shand stands in front of the Chief bolt upright and confident for the first time, daring him to disagree.

'Do what you think is necessary but keep it inside the law.'

'As far as I'm concerned, Sir, there is no other way.'

With that he leaves the Chief's office, not slamming the door this time.

In the holding cell Doctor Cole is talking to his solicitor.

'You were very silent up there. What am I paying you for?'

'The only advice I can give you is to tell the truth. It's the only way. The police are not stupid and if you're connected in any way to these murders, then it's too big for me to handle. I don't think I can help.'

'If I tell them that the number was mine what can they do to me?'

'Are you telling me that it is your number?'

'Yes, it is. But I leant it to a friend to use. Will they believe me?'

'You will have to tell them this friend's name. They wont let it go. You know this don't you? This is way to big. Three murders. The police won't stop until they have all those involved in custody.'

Doctor Cole is looking at the floor turning his hands over and over and rubbing the back of his neck feeling completely alone and vulnerable, trying to think what to do next. For the first time in his life he's frightened.

CHAPTER TWENTY-SIX

Shand takes a moment to relax in his office, pouring a coffee and noticing his hands are not shaking. Sergeant Walker enters the room with a pile of paperwork in his arms.

'What have you got there, Robert?'

'Everything we have so far on the case, Sir. I want to go over it before we interview Doctor Cole again.'

'Very well, how long will you need?'

'A couple of hours should do.'

'Fine with me. Doctor Cole can sit in his cell and contemplate his future. He's not going anywhere until I get a satisfactory answer from him.'

Shand's desk phone rings he lifts the receiver placing it to his ear.

'DCI Shand.'

'Mr Shand, I'm Mr Gasper. Doctor Cole's solicitor. Could I come to your office? I have some information I think you should hear.'

'Okay, come up now, the desk Sergeant will show you the way. Tell him I said it's okay for you to see me.'

Shand looks to Sergeant Walker.

'Doctor Cole's solicitor is on his way up with some

information.'

'Do you want me to stay, Sir?'

'Yes, Robert, I do. And I think we should tape the conversation as well. Can you see to that please?'

Shand, Walker and Mr Gasper are sitting at the glass oval coffee table in Shand's office. 'I'm taping this conversation, Mr Gasper. Do you have any objections?'

'None what so ever, Mr Shand. I'm only going to convey what Doctor Cole asked me to. Nothing more at this point.'

'Very well, Mr Gasper, please continue?'

'Doctor Cole has admitted that the mobile phone number relating to the warning messages that Miss Christi received is his. However he is very adamant about the fact that he lent it to a friend some weeks before any of these murders took place. And further more he is very resolute about proclaiming his innocence.'

'Interesting, Mr Gasper. If this is true, I will need the name of this so called friend. It's vitally important that we speak to him. Assuming it is a 'he'?

'In my opinion, Mr Shand, yes, it is.'

Shand holds up his hand gesturing Mr Gasper to stop speaking.

'Mr Gasper, I'm not interested in your opinion. I'm only interested in facts. Now, if it's true what Doctor Cole said about his so called friend then I want a name. Do you understand?'

'Perfectly, Mr Shand. I will have to convey our conversation to him.'

'We can all do that now, Mr Gasper. I have every intension of re-interviewing Doctor Cole this afternoon, right now in fact. Shall we?'

Back in the interview room, Doctor Cole is looking extremely anxious.

'Good afternoon, Doctor Cole. I am going to restart the tape and continue with the interview. Do you understand me?'

He nods his head as if to say yes. He seems embarrassed to look Shand in the eye.

'Interview commenced at eighteen thirty hours, the same day, the same people are present as before. Now Doctor Cole, new evidence has come to light by way of your admission to being the registered owner of the mobile phone number in question. Is that true?'

'Yes, it's true.'

'Very good Doctor. Now I'm led to believe you lent this number to a friend before any of these murders took place. Is that true?'

'Yes, it's true.'

'Now, all I need to know is the name of the person you lent this number to.'

Doctor Cole looks at Shand, then at Mr Gasper and finally at the floor. He is overwhelmed and can't bring himself to say the name.

'I'm waiting, Doctor. The sooner you give me the name the sooner you can go home.'

'It's not that simple, you don't understand.'

'Then explain it to me, please, so I can understand. You seem to forget, Doctor that this phone number directly links, who ever used it, to the first murder and possibly the other two. As these murders are linked, for that reason alone, you have a public and moral duty to give me the information I'm asking for.'

Doctor Cole leans back in his chair, takes a beep breath and exhales feeling very distraught.

'Very well, Mr Shand, as you insist. His name is Arthur Ambrose. I gave him the chip about nine months ago. He said his one had become corrupt and he needed a number for work when he was out delivering his meat.

'Mr Ambrose, the local butcher? Am I right Doctor?'

'Yes, Mr Shand. That's correct.'

'Thank you, Doctor Cole. Interview terminated at precisely nineteen fifteen hours the same day.'

Shand leans forward to switch off the tape recorder, stands up and moves towards the door of the interview room.

'Mr Shand, I take it my client is free to go?' asks Mr Gasper the solicitor.

Shand stands by the door with one hand on the handle looking first at Mr Gaspar and then at Doctor Cole. He seems deep in thought.

'No, Mr Gasper. I'm sorry, not just yet.'

'I don't understand. My client has given you the information you required. Why do you need to hold him any longer?'

'Because, Mr Gaspar, I have reason to believe that Doctor Cole is directly involved. Once I have spoken to Mr Ambrose and established his innocence then I will consider releasing him untill then Dr Cole stayes here.'

Shand turns to his Sergeant.

'Sergeant Walker, take Doctor Cole back to the holding cell and make sure he's offered refreshment?'

Doctor Cole immediately starts shouting

'You can't hold me like I'm some sort of criminal. I've given you what you asked for. I demand you release me now:'

Shand, not reacting to Doctor Cole's outburst, walks back to his office leaving Doctor Cole screaming and shouting.

Before he has a chance to sit at his desk the phone rings. It's the Chief Constable.

'Mr Shand, would you spare me a few moments, please?'

Shand doesn't bother knocking anymore; he walks straight in with a look of frostiness about him. He sits down, opens the file on the red leather top of the Chief's desk waiting for the Chief to speak.

'I've just had Doctor Coles solicitor here demanding his release. Why are you still holding him? You have the information you require.'

'Because, Sir,' the Chief detects a note of sarcasm in his voice, 'I have reason to believe he is connected to the murders in some way. If I let him go, he'll do one of two things.'

'And what might that be Mr Shand?'

'I believe he will either disappear or he will contact Arthur

Ambrose warning him we are on to him. If he disappears it would put us back to square one. I'm not prepared to take that risk. This is the closest we have come to finding these murderers and possibly Daniel Winter. I can hold him for thirty-six hours and that's exactly what I propose to do. Please do not think you can outrank me on this, Sir. You know what my response will be, don't you?'

The Chief looks at Shand with his hands in his favoured position as if in prayer. For the first time he feels he's loosing control of the case.

'Very well, Mr Shand. See to it. I hope for your sake you're right about Doctor Cole because if you are wrong the ramifications will be unbelievable.'

Shand doesn't bother to acknowledge the Chief. He walks out of his office leaving the door wide open. The Chief picks up his phone and dials a number. While he's waiting for the connection he closes the door.

Arthur Ambrose is busy in his shop cutting a slice of beef for a customer. The phone is ringing in the background. He looks up and shouts:

'Get that, will you? He's looking at his apprentice who is putting trays of meat in the cold room. He looks back to his customer grinning.

'Sorry about that. He's a bit gormless but a good kid.'

He wraps up the beef.

'There you are. Anything else?'

The customer puts the package in her bag.

'No thanks, that's all for today.'

'Right you are then, see you soon. Good day to you.'

The apprentice comes back into the shop looking puzzled.

'What's wrong? Your girlfriend just chucked you?'

He gently slaps him on his back and walks to the back room to make a cup of tea. His apprentice follows him in still looking strange. Ambrose is standing holding the boiling kettle to his mug, looks round and says:

'What's wrong with you? Don't worry there's plenty more fish in the sea.'

'It wasn't my girlfriend. It was a man.'

Ambrose puts the steaming kettle down slowly staring at his apprentice.

'What man? What did he say?'

'He said the police are on to you. Get out now.'

Ambrose standing in the room ridged with fear runs to the front of the shop looking up and down the street. He walks back inside locks the door, runs to the back room shouting at his apprentice:

'Get the fuck out of here. Now.'

He grabs his keys, locks the back door and runs to his van, starting the engine, tyres howling as he races away.

CHAPTER TWENTY-SEVEN

The Chief replaces the phone and sits back in his soft leather chair, which makes a soft groaning sound as if it is complaining about his weight. He is deep in thought. At the same time Doctor Cole is in the custody suite returning the handset to its cradle.

Shand and Walker are on their way to Arthur Ambrose's shop with a uniformed constable sitting up front next to the driver. As they pull up outside they can see the apprentice standing by the front door scratching his head in bewilderment.

Shand gets out of the car first running with pace closely followed by Sergeant Walker and the uniformed constable. The apprentice is talking loudly on his mobile phone, his arm shaking uncontrollably above his head. Shand stops in front of him pulling his warrant card from the inside pocket of his jacket almost pushing it in his face. The apprentice leans back to avoid it.

'I'm Detective Chief Inspector Shand. What's your name?'

The apprentice looks at the warrant card then up to Shand.

'I'm Billy Caine. What's going on?'

As Shand is talking to him, Walker and the uniformed constable are trying to open the shop door. Walker turns round shouting:

'It's locked.'

Shand hollers back:

'Try the back, and fast.'

He turns back to Billy.

'Now, listen carefully, Billy, this is extremely important.

Where is Mr Ambrose?'

'Dunno. He just ran out the back door to his van and roared off.'

'Didn't he tell you where he was going?'

'No. One minute he was making a cup of tea the next he was gone after I told him about the phone call I took for him.'

'What phone call?'

'He was busy with a customer, the phone was ringing, so he asked me to answer it. I thought it would be a customer wanting to make an order.'

'Okay, Billy, now think very hard who it was on the phone? And what did he say?'

'He didn't say his name, he just said. 'The police are on to you, get out now.'

Walker appears by Shand's side.

'The back door is locked as well, and the van's missing.'

Shand is glued to the pavement outside the butcher's shop, his heads spinning. It all spirals out of control. Someone is always one step ahead of him and he doesn't have a clue who, but he intends to find out. And there is one man who can tell him. He asks the Constable to take Billy's details and stay by the shop in case Ambrose returns.

Arthur Ambrose is speeding like a madman; one hand on the steering wheel while the other is holding the phone to his ear. He is driving but he doesn't know where to, any direction will do as long as it is away from town and the police. The mobile's battery is low so there is no signal.

'Fuck it.'

He throws it on the seat beside him and it bounces to the floor. His foot pushes the accelerator pedal harder and the van's front lifts slightly as it heads out of town.

Shand is back at the police station and he heads straight for the custody suite. Sergeant Manning is at his desk.

'Sergeant, I need to speak to Doctor Cole. It's urgent. Can you bring him to interview room number one, pleases?'

'I'm sorry, Sir. He's gone.'

'What do you mean, he's gone? I didn't authorise his release.'

'No, Sir. But the Chief Constable did about half an hour ago.'

Sergeant Manning shows Shand the release papers signed by the Chief.

Shand turns and runs through the corridors of the police station to the Chief's office. On the stairs, he climbs two steps at a time pushing several people out of the way as he rushes past them. He does not bother to knock; he pushes the door so hard it crashes against the Chief's coat stand almost causing it to fall. The Chief is standing with the phone receiver in his hand. Shand is out of breath and it takes him a few seconds to compose himself. The Chief places the reviver back into its cradle keeping a watchful eye on Shand.

'What can I do for you, DCI Shand?'

'You've released Doctor Cole against my strict instructions. Why?'

'First of all, Mr Shand, remember to whom you're speaking. I wont have you bursting into my office demanding answers from me. Do you understand?'

Shand still trying to control his breathing, he looks at his watch.

'I apologies, Sir, but I must insist. Why did you let him go?'

'On the advice of his lawyer. It was very risky holding him on such insubstantial evidence. He's at his surgery if you need to speak to him.'

'Did you know Sir, Arthur Ambrose received a phone call warning him that we were coming and wanted to speak to him?'

'No, Mr Shand, of course not, how could I?'

'Well, somebody did, he's disappeared, locked his shop and fled leaving his apprentice standing on the street with no explanation. Why would he do that? And now I find out that the only person who might possibly help has also gone.'

'He's not 'gone' as you put it, he's at his surgery or at home. I'm sure he will be happy to explain anything you ask.

'I hope so, Sir, for all our sakes, I hope so.'

Back in his office, Shand picks up the phone and dials the surgery. He looks at Sergeant Walker who is pouring a coffee for him.

'Extra milk, Sir?'

Shand grins, as if to say 'yes, please.' Someone answers the

175

phone.

'Doctor Cole's surgery?'

'Hello. This is DCI Shand. I need to speak the Doctor Cole, please. It's an emergency.'

'I'm sorry, he's not here today. He said he would be out all day.'

'Then can you reach him on his mobile, please. It's extremely urgent.'

'Hold on, I'll try.'

The phone goes quiet. Shand takes a sip of his coffee.

'Jesus, Robert. Are you trying to get me drunk?'

'Medicinal purposes, Sir.'

A voice comes back on the line.

'I'm sorry. His mobile seems to be switched off.'

Shand returns the handset to its cradle, looks up at the ceiling then down to his mug of coffee. He takes an enormous mouthful, hoping the whiskey in it will help.

He drops into his chair. Walker eyes him cautiously.

'What's wrong, Sir?'

Shand looks across at Walker. He always liked working with him. He is probably one of the few people he can really trust but he realises one day he will get promotion and move onto another police station.

'Robert, it looks like we have two people on the run. First, our Mr Ambrose and now it looks like the good Doctor has vanished as well.'

176

'You're kidding me, Sir. Who'd have thought it? Doctor Cole a mass murderer?'

'I can't be sure yet, Robert. But it's starting to look like he and Ambrose are connected. Plus we need to find the other three concerned.'

'How do you know there are three more?'

'Remember, Miss Collins, the medium, she said Mark Bruley spoke to her, telling her there were five men there when he was murdered. Five men in blood red robes with long daggers hanging from a thick leather belt.'

'It gives me the creeps just thinking about it, Sir.'

'Me too, Robert, but the fact remains we have five men out there somewhere killing people for whatever crazy reason they think justifies their actions. And we had one of them in the cells and the Chief, in all his wisdom, let him walk straight out the front door.'

'Do you really believe Doctor Cole is one of them, Sir?'

'Yes, I do. All along something has been bugging me about his behaviour on the three occasions he did the post mortems. He was too unperturbed about the post mortems for my liking, he just seemed to take it all in his stride. Plus, his outburst at Doctor Simmonds the day we came back from the castle.'

'But I checked him out, he's clean. I found nothing, not even a parking ticket.'

'I know, but that doesn't mean he's not involved somehow. You know what they say don't you, Robert?'

'No, Sir. What?'

'The quiet ones are the worst.'

'Are you going to tell the Chief what has happened, Sir?'

'To be perfectly frank, Robert, I don't give a shit if he knows or not. He's the cretin that let a mass murderer walk out the front door of this police station today. I'm going home. We've done all we can for now. The call is out for these two. We'll find them sooner or later.'

'What about Daniel Winter, Sir? He's still missing.'

'I remember, Robert, but we still have no idea where to look. I hope now this new evidence has come to light, wherever they have hidden him, they won't harm him. Remember there are three of this group left, and I get the feeling that Doctor Cole is the headman, so without his say the others will sit tight and do nothing.'

'I hope you're right, Sir.'

'Me too. Good night, Robert, see you in the morning.'

Arthur Ambrose is panicking, every car he sees, he thinks, it is the police. He still does not know what to do or where to go. He has been driving for many hours. It is getting dark and he is feeling exhausted. It started to rain an hour ago and now it is pouring down in torrents making it difficult to see ahead of him. Suddenly his phone bursts into life, he had forgotten all about it. The pulsating glow from the screen shows him where it is.

'Shit,' he thinks to himself, I can't reach it, it is too far for him to reach. With one hand on the steering wheel he tries to reach down for the phone. The ringing is getting louder and louder, filling him with a rage that makes his head explode. He stretches a little further fingers just touching the phone.

'Got it.' As he looks up he sees furious headlights from a juggernaut searing down on him. He yells, pulls at the steering wheel hard to the left but it is too late. The colossal juggernaut is on top of his van pushing him backwards. All he hears are tyres shuddering and screaming like demons on the tarmac as the other driver tries to control his vehicle. Suddenly a tyre bursts sounding like a bomb exploding, making the juggernaut list to one side. He hears the klaxons of the lorry wailing. Heat is pouring out of the spotlights from the front of the juggernaut, turning the inside of his van yellow absorbing him, sending him blind. Then there is the sound of metal twisting and air breaks howling. The contact is extremely violent as the two vehicles meet head on. Ambrose grips his steering wheel hard, his knuckles turning white. He holds in his breath hoping it is a nightmare he will wake from. Then he is aware of a loud explosion and the sound of shattering glass. His van is pushed backwards with such velocity that Ambrose is propelled forwards, bashing his head on the steering wheel. The van wrapping itself round an enormous oak tree abruptly stops. Finally darkness and silence surrounds him.

Both vehicles lay still, steam pouring from the shattered radiators. Ambrose's van engine is roaring ferociously as his foot is crushed between the accelerator and the foot well. The force of the impact was so severe it is difficult to tell one vehicle front from the other. The juggernauts driver's cab has completely turned on its side ripping all the compressor lines from the rest of the vehicle, which hang swinging, hissing and crying into the night. There is petrol and diesel escaping from both vehicles, the rivers of fuel are about to meet. The juggernaut's driver screams as fire surrounds him. He tries to claw his way out of his cab but he is trapped between the steering wheel and the dashboard. He sees the two streams of fuel about to come together, the heat and force from the fire choking him. He feels his hair singeing and burning on his head, the skin on his hands melting from the heat as his bones start to appear he can't believe what he is seeing.

CHAPTER TWENTY-EIGHT

Neal Annabel and Molly are enjoying a delicious dinner. They are talking about all sorts of different things. Neal asks both of them to talk about anything except the murder case. It is starting to overtake his life.

'So, Molly, tell me about your exams. I'm sorry I didn't ask you sooner. How do you think you did?'

'Okay, I'm pretty sure I'll have passed most subjects. As long as I get a. Desmond, I'll be happy.'

Neal and Annabel appear extremely baffled. Molly sees the looks on their faces and giggles.

'A Desmond,' she repeats staring at both of them tossing her head back crying with laughter.

'I'm sorry Molly, we haven't got a clue what you're talking about.'

'My God, both of you, which cave have you been hibernating in? A Desmond is a two-two. You know? Desmond Tutu. A 'two two' is a pretty good grade to get in a degree.'

Neal looks at Annabel.

'Pour me another glass of wine, please, sweetheart a big one.

'Sure. I think I'll join you if you don't mind.'

The rest of the evening is spent with more teasing from Molly. She is beginning to see her father in a different light since he met Annabel. He is more relaxed and happy. Much more like his old self before her mother was killed. She sits on the armchair watching him and Annabel laughing and joking gently pushing and shoving each other holding each other like two lovers should. She looks at her watch.

'Okay you two, I'm going up to my room to read for a while. I'll leave you the washing up, that'll keep you busy for a while'.

'Okay, precious, sweet dreams.'

Neal looks into Annabel's eyes with wanting.

'It's just us now'

The traffic police arrive on the scene. The night sky is filled with blue and red flashing lights from police cars, fire engines and ambulances. Fire fighters hurry to put out the flames before they can free the occupants of the vehicles. The sound of the hydraulic cutting equipment fills the air with a crude penetrating shrill as they frantically cut the roofs off both vehicles. A piercing scream from one of the vehicles is ear splitting. A paramedic runs towards the sound, yelling to his colleagues to follow him. The Chief of the fire department turns to the Inspector of traffic police with a look of disbelief.

'My God, if one of these two has survived, I dread to think what condition he or she will be in. This is the worst road accident I've seen in years.'

The paramedics work frenziedly on their injured drivers, crawling over the vehicle trying to get closer. The rain has stopped, making conditions easier for them to work. The enormous oak tree stands firm, its leaves and branches blowing, moaning and complaining in the wind, allowing droplets of water to fall on the paramedics while they try desperately to save a life. The screams die down as the morphine kicks in, allowing the medical team work faster. With no one struggling anymore to hinder them, they free their man carrying him to the ambulance on a stretcher with one medic trying to run along aside, holding high the bottle of saline drip, The ground is slippery with petrol, diesel and rain all mixed together. Two breakdown vehicles arrive to take away the wreckage. Nevertheless the juggernaut's main body has to stay where it is until a larger recovery vehicle can come in the morning. They concentrate on the driver's cab only. A black body bag is placed gently in the back of another ambulance. One of the paramedics looks physically shaken by what he witnessed. The fire crew are busy covering the ground with foam around both vehicles to make sure no more fires can start. All the emergency services move away slowly, their work finished.

Early the following morning, Shand is driving himself to the police station in his Beetle, his favourite CD playing. He always loved the 'Monkees' 'Daydream Believer'. He joins in the chorus, his fingers tapping the steering wheel to the rhythm of the music. He looks in the rear view mirror telling himself: 'I must really take singing lessons.' As he stops in the police station car park he notices several motorway police vehicles and the chief of the Fire services' car parked along side. He walks in through the front door to see if he can speak to someone. It is unusual to see so many traffic cars; they normally park in their own spaces in another part of the building. The night duty Sergeant is still at his desk talking to the chief of the Fire service. They are both drinking large mugs of steaming hot tea.

'Morning, Bob. Morning, Ray. Did I miss something?'

The night Sergeant should have been off duty three hours ago. There is stubble appearing on his chin and dark circles under his eyes.

'Morning, Mr Shand. Yes, there was a terrible accident last night. Two vehicles involved, a domestic van and a HGV, a forty tonner. We have one fatality and one in a extremely serious way in the hospital, in a coma.'

'Anyone I should know about, Sergeant?'

'The driver of the juggernaut was pronounced dead at the

scene. His name was Benoit Masson from France. We're still trying to locate the transport company to inform them, apparently they're somewhere in Paris. The fire service managed to retrieve his overnight bag from the driver's cab before it went up in flames. The other driver was in a black van. His name is Arthur Ambrose. He's in a critical condition at St Mary's. There's a constable keeping guard outside his room.'

Shand feels like he has been hit on his head with a sledgehammer, a shiver is running down his spine the hair on the back of his neck starts to raise up. He feels as if his shoes are glued to the floor, he doesn't know what to do or say next. The Fire chief moves closer to Shand looking particularly solemn, the smell of the fire still evident on his florescent jacket. Shand looks at him open-mouthed, eyes wide open in disbelief.

'Mr Shand, I've been in the Fire service for twenty-nine years. I have seen some horrific things in my time. But last night I watched a man burn to death. I stood there looking at him clawing at the windshield in his cab literally fighting for his life. Above all the commotion around me, I could hear him screams for help. Unfortunately we were driven back by the intensity of the blaze; his fuel tanks had burst into flames. There was diesel, and petrol from the other vehicle, everywhere. He also had flammable liquid in the rear tanker of the juggernaut. We couldn't get close enough to save him. By the time we got to the scene the fire was like an inferno. It took us three hours to get both the blazes under control. The last thing I remember was his face pressed against the glass, the look of horror as he glared in disbelief at me. I could see his mouth moving. Then the smoke engulfed him and he disappeared in a thick black fog. His body was unrecognisable by the time we got inside the vehicle.'

Shand feels his mouth moving but no words would come out. He is like a goldfish in a glass bowel. For the first time since his wife's funeral he crosses himself. He has to force himself to speak.

'You said the driver of the other vehicle was called Arthur Ambrose?'

'Yes, Sir. He got off only marginally better.'

'How do you mean?'

The Fire chief sees Sergeant Manning entering the police station and going to sit at his desk. Shand asks the Fire chief to continue.

'The driver of the other vehicle is alive. But only just. The paramedics had to amputate one of his legs just below the knee to free him. His foot was jammed between the pedals. The force of the impact was so severe; it pushed most of the van's driving compartment back several inches. He has head injuries and multiple fractures. He's been in a coma since we freed him, that's why he's better off. But when he wakes it will be horrendous for him.'

Shand thanks him, walks off to his office, his head whirling and feeling as if there were a dark mist surrounding him. His vision is starting to blur, he rubs his eyes with his fingers. Sergeant Walker is working at his desk turns round.

'You look like you've seen a ghost, Sir. What's wrong?'

'I've just been with the Fire Chief. He told me about last night's crash. It was horrific.'

'Yes, Sir, I had a look at the cad report a moment ago. I recognised one name.'

'Me too, Robert. He's at St Mary's in a coma so there's no need to rush there. He's going nowhere for a long time.'

'You need a coffee, Sir.'

Okay, but with real milk, please. Not your special kind, it's far too early for that.'

Shand eases into his chair, staring at the pile of files on his desk, a mug of steaming coffee beside him. The door opens softly; the groaning hinge alerts him. He looks up to see the Chief Constable coming to stand in front of him with a sheet of paper in his hand waving it about like it were a winning lottery ticket.

'Have you seen this, Mr Shand?'

'If you're referring to the road traffic accident of last night then, yes, I've just spoken to the Fire chief.'

'Well, at least you have found one of your people you've been searching for.'

Shand looks up to the Chief who is still standing. He had not bothered to ask him to sit.

'And the other one, Sir? You remember? The one you let walk out of here yesterday.'

The Chief raises his hand curling his fingers in a fist, gently placing it to his mouth giving a little cough.

'Hmm, yes, well, we are still looking for him. I have put a

watch on his house and one on his surgery. And I have circulated his vehicle details to the ports and airports. We'll find him.'

'Thank you, Sir. Most helpful, I'm sure, but what about our missing person? For all we know he could already be dead. We now know of two people involved. But I can't speak to either of them can I? So I'm not much better off, am I, Sir?'

The Chief is swaying gently from one foot to the other as if he were uncomfortable standing but Shand still does not invite him to sit.

'Very well, Mr Shand. I'll let you get on. Do your best.'

With that he turns and walks out of Shand's office vanishing into the maze of corridors. Shand sits back in his chair looking at his coffee, which has gone cold.

Harvey Ventura is busy in the bar restocking bottles in his coolers. The large flat screen television, which he uses for all the sporting events, is switched on with the local news in the background. He is not taking much notice only giving it a cursory look every now and then. He needs to be ready for opening time. He listens to the weather report. More rain and high winds, 'Bloody marvellous' he whispers. It is still summer and he has only been able to use his beer garden twice for BBQs so far. As he is wiping down the tables and setting them for the lunch trade, he hears a news flash. Looking up he sees the charred remains of two burnt out vehicles and a pretty female reporter standing at the scene holding an umbrella in one hand and her microphone in the other. She is describing the events of night before. Ventura stops to watch. The reporter looks familiar. He cannot quite remember where he has seen her before. As she is giving her report, the hood on her overcoat blows off her head revelling beautiful long flowing red hair. Ventura says out loud: 'that's Annabel Christi from the Local Gazette. What a stunner.' He looks round and realizes he is alone in his bar. Just as he decides to carry on preparing the tables for lunch he hears two names. The first one is Benoit Masson. This means nothing to him but then he hears the other one, Arthur Ambrose. He turns back to the television staring at it not believing what he has just heard. He drops his tray of cutlery and runs to the phone. He is sweating as he dials, mumbling to himself:

'How the fuck did he get involved in an accident. Where was he going that time of night?'

As there is no answer, he slams the receiver down, breathing hard thinking: 'I'll call the Master, he'll know what to do. Again he dials a number. This time someone answers.

'Doctor Cole's surgery.'

'Can I speak to Doctor Cole, please? It's an emergency.'

The voice comes back.

'I'm sorry but Doctor Cole is indisposed. I can put you through to the locum if you wish?'

Ventura, gripping the hand piece holding it up in the air, is not sure whether to speak or hang up.

The voice returns.

'Are you still there, caller?'

He slams the hand piece down, nearly pulling the phone off the wall. He has to take a deep breath to calm down. He stares at the optics then he looks at his watch.

'It is only nine thirty but I think I need a whisky.'

He takes a glass and pours a double.

Clancy Belet is in his office going over the last day's trading. Ever since his secretary asked for a radio, it is on in her office. He can hear classical music playing and he always tries to guess which composer is playing.

'Vivaldi,' he says to himself.

His secretary comes in with a pile of paperwork, which she puts carefully on his desk. As she walks out she turns and says:

'Dreadful news about that crash last night. One of the victims was our local butcher, wasn't it? What's his name? Arthur Ambrose. Yes, that's it, I remember now. A charming man. I always used his shop because he would often put in a little extra. I think he had a bit of a shine for me.'

She returns to her office chuckling.

The desk phone rings and he picks it up.

'Belet.'

'It's Harvey. Have you seen the news this morning about the crash? Arthur was involved. He's at St Mary's.'

'Yes, just now my secretary was talking about it. It came on the radio. Of course I didn't react. Have you contacted the Master?'

'I tried. The surgery told me he's indisposed. Whatever that's supposed to mean.'

'Listen, don't do anything. I'll call Frank. I think we had better get together and talk about this. Don't forget about our 'man'. Has anyone been to see him today?'

'I was going to go later when my staff arrive.'

'Okay, go anyway, give him some water and make sure he's still alive. If he isn't just leave him where he is. It will take forever for anyone to find him.'

'Okay. But don't come to the pub, let's meet somewhere different.'

'Where do you suggest?

'The beach, by Merlin's cove. There's a small inlet and a cave. No one will see or hear us there.'

'All right, be there at four. We'll be waiting.'

Ventura hangs up the phone. As he turns round his barmaid Jenny is staring at him. He only gave her the job because of her enormous breasts. He thought it would be good for business. She is a hopeless barmaid but she looks good in a low cut top revelling ample cleavage, and a tight mini skirt. Her long legs seem to go on forever he always enjoys watching her behind the bar.

'Jesus, you frightened me. I didn't hear you come in. How long have you been standing there?'

'You were obviously deep in discussion. I've been here for a few minutes. Where do you want me?'

Ventura looks aghast at Jenny; all sorts of images are going through his mind.

'How do you mean?'

'I'm talking about where you want me. Behind the bar or waitressing in the restaurant?'

'Oh, okay, stay here behind the bar today. I have to go out for a while. I'll be about an hour. Take care of things for me, will you?'

Leaving Jenny in the bar he puts on his jacket and walks towards the back door to the car park. As he is heading towards his car, lighting a cigarette, his mobile rings. The screen shows it is Frank de Caux. He doesn't know if he should answer. He stops by his car smoking his cigarette looking at his phone. Not answering he puts his phone in his pocket, uses his remote to unlock his car and he calmly drives away heading to the north coast.

CHAPTER TWENTY-NINE

Daniel Winter is becoming delirious from lack of food. The bottles of water help him but it has been several days, he can't remember exactly how long, he has been held here. Time means nothing to him anymore. The men, whoever they are, took everything from him leaving him in just his underwear he is frozen at night. The cave where he is being kept is constantly wet. The sound of the tide ebbing and flowing is starting to drive him mad, the noise never changing with waves crashing against the rocks. The chain holding him is only ten feet long; restricting his movements it is thick and rusty. Every time he tries to move, the leg iron cuts deeper into his ankle. He discovers what it feels like to experience extreme solitude. Suddenly he sees a silhouette in the distance walking towards him. His eyes are blurred because of the lack of food and ceaseless darkness in the cave. As the figure gets closer he can make out a bulky man swiftly heading towards him. He hears a voice. He cries into the darkness. 'Help. Help. Please, help me?' The figure being closer he can now see who it is. Daniel Winter cries out to him:

'For God's sake, help me, I'm dying here.'

He is sobbing as he speaks, his bottom lip trembles, tears run down his cheeks. He is shaking with fear. He pulls his forearm across his face, sniffing. He tries to sit up pulling his knees up to his chest. His underwear is soiled because he is finding it hard to control his bowels. His torturer is squatting in front of him, looking penetratingly into his eyes.

'Still with us then?'

Ventura grins at him rubbing his head more or less in an act of kindness. Daniel Winter is too scared to look him in the eye. Staring at the ground he whispers.

'Please, let me go.'

Harvey Ventura inclines his head to Winters mouth.

'What did you say, sonny?'

Winter does not reply. He cannot control his body's quaking with terror.

'You want me to let you go, do you? Is that what you said?'

Daniel Winter too scared to look at him whispers:

'Yes, let me go.'

Harvey Ventura's expression changes from one of amusement to one of savagery. He eyes squint, his mouth tenses, his forehead creases and his voice drops to a chilling deep drawl.

'You're going fucking nowhere, boy.'

He puts the bottle of water down in front of Daniel Winter looking at him with an expression of revulsion. Winters bowels discharge in his underwear again. Ventura leans in and talks close to Daniel Winters ear.

'Don't forget we know what you've been up to, you filthy fucking arsehole. You used to be a big man, didn't you? Or so you presumed, your little army of thieves mugging old people for their pension money. Prostituting young girls, as young as twelve years old, raping most of them yourself, for your own amusement, before you sent them out on the street, usually drugged so they wouldn't object. While you sat in the Celtic Knot every night like some sort of fucking king in your own castle. I'm the landlord of the Celtic Knot and I had to look at you every night getting pissed on the money of others. It makes me fucking sick just to look at you.'

Ventura stands up.

'Look how the big man has fallen. You're going to die here slowly, painfully, agonizingly and all alone. No one will give a fuck about you by the time anyone finds you. You will be so decomposed only your teeth will tell who you were. Believe me it's better than what we had in store for you. Your death will be much less painful than the others we took care of.

The cynic smirk returns to Ventura's face. He turns round, walks off not saying another word. Daniel Winter pulls his knees up to his chin sobbing hysterically. No one can hear his cries, the noise of the crashing waves drown out his sobs.

Harvey Ventura pulls up in the car park of the Celtic Knot. He sees Clancy Belet and Frank de Caux standing by the back door. He walks toward them with a grin on his face still pleased with his tête-à-tête with Daniel Winter.

'Morning, you two'

They both stand there not responding.

'What's wrong? You two have faces like shit.'

They both look at each other then back at Ventura.

'Don't you read the newspapers?'

Ventura looks puzzled.

'Of course I do, why?'

'Then you'll know about the Master, wont you?'

'How do you mean?'

'He was arrested. Fortunately he was realised. We don't know what he told Shand, and now he's gone missing.'

'I watched the news this morning. That gorgeous red head was on the television this morning, great pair of tits. I would love to get my hands on then.'

'Stop fooling around, what are we going to do? We've been left in the shit big time. What about the candidate Winter? What are we going to do with him?'

'Don't worry about him, I've just been there. He's still with

194

us so to speak, I suggest we just leave him; he's never going to escape from those manacles. We just carry on as normal. No one has any idea what we've been doing, or who we are.'

'You seem very calm about all this. I'm not so sure with the Master out there somewhere and Ambrose in hospital. What happens when he comes round?'

Ventura looks at both of them the expression of revulsion returning; both De Caux and Belet take a step back from him.

'When he comes round he keeps quiet for his sake. Or I'll go and visit him to make sure he doesn't say anything stupid. I'm not going to prison for no one, understand?' Ventura's stare pierces into them to the point they are terrified.

'Now fuck off both of you, I have a pub to run.'

Doctor Cole makes his way carefully to his boat moored in Torquay. He has had it for two years now, only using it at weekends and occasional holidays. It is a majestic Sea Ray 270 DA. It is more than 8 meters with a powerful 4.3 litre engine. He has been hiding it in a disused boat shed, using a small family run local store for food.

He is casually strolling down to the harbour, stopping every few meters to make certain there is no one else around. No one knows about his boat, not even his wife since he also used it for other lady friends on evenings of covetousness. He registered it under a false name to keep his real identity secret. When he is sure there is no one to see him, he slips aboard, releases the ropes and starts the engine steadily and soundlessly. Keeping the engine at a low rev he drifts away into the night heading south, for the coast of France.

DCI Shand, and Sergeant Walker are both at their desks burrowing their way through the mountains of paper work the case has generated so far. Walker turn in his chair.

'Sir?'

'What is it, Robert?'

'I've been checking on Daniel Winter. You know he wasn't such a nice character after all. We have nothing on him that's why we couldn't understand why he was taken. I've been asking around some of our more 'undesirable' citizens. He was actually quiet the kingpin in the area.

'Tell me, Sergeant.'

'Well, there's a long list. Prostitution, drugs, money lending, protection on small local businesses, buying and selling some very dubious cars and motorbikes, false MOT insurance write-offs, the list goes on and on, Sir.'

'Sounds like we had our very own Al Capone right on our doorstep. Why did we never have him in for a chat?'

'That's the problem, Sir. He ran a very tight ship so to speak. All his people would never grass on him, they were far too petrified of what he would do to them if he found out they were talking to us.'

'Such as?'

'Apparently one of his guys tried to keep some of the takings, more than he should have. Daniel Winter found out and went looking for him. When he found him the first thing he did was to kill his dog with a machete while he was watching, then he dowsed him with petrol and set it alight. Daniel Winter put the flames out before they could do any real damage saying if it happened again, he wouldn't be so fast to put out the fire.'

'Nice guy. So how did these people, who have been executing the others, get to know about him?'

'Well, as I said, Sir, I've been talking to local business people telling them he had vanished. This made them open up and talk. It's surprising how chatty they became when they heard he'd gone. Maybe some of these business people are also our killers?'

'Good work, Sergeant. What now?'

'To be honest, Sir, I'm not really sure. He has literally disappeared, and we don't have a clue where to look. It's the same as with the others, once the locals know they have disappeared, they don't care if these criminals never came back.'

Shand gazes at Sergeant Walker with a vacant stare.

'Something wrong, Sir?'

'Just thinking, Robert, what if the local butcher is one of our people? And Doctor Cole? It's all starting to fit. If this is true, then there are still three more out there somewhere, remember? Miss Collins said there were five men dressed in the same manner.

CHAPTER THIRTY

Shand is deep in thought, strumming his fingers on his desk. He looks up.

'Tell me, Robert, if Doctor Cole is innocent, then why has he gone missing? And why did Arthur Ambrose panic after receiving a phone call? Remember his shop assistant said he shot out of there like a bat out of hell after that call. The mobile phone number connected to Doctor Cole? And what about the black van belonging to Arthur Ambrose? There's a lot of loose ends, but they're slowly coming together.'

'I understand, Sir. But we're still not much closer to finding the murderers and Daniel Winter. These people must be getting worried now two of them are gone. What will the other three do with the victim?'

'I dread to think. If they start to panic there's no telling what they might do. God knows they're violent enough as it is.'

'Come with me, Robert. I think we should go and visit Mr Ambrose, see if he's come round yet. As usual they wont give any information over the phone.'

St Mary's hospital is a large building comprising five floors and four wings. It's over a hundred years old and in the shape of a horseshoe. It has that very characteristic smell that all hospitals seem to have, the smell of disinfectant and iodoform, and the sweet smell of iodine.

Arthur Ambrose is in the trauma wing, where accident victims are put after road tragedies. Shand and Walker find the uniformed constable sitting outside room 301 just as the receptionist told them. The surgeon is just about to enter the room. Shand identifies himself.

'Morning, Mr Bolan. How is Mr Ambrose? I really need to talk to him.'

'I'm afraid that wont be possible for quite some time, he's still in a coma. Even if he wasn't I would have induced one, his injuries are so severe he couldn't have handled the pain. I can't be sure if he'll ever come out of it, his whole viscera is the wrong way round, this is the laymen's term for everything inside him, all his internal organs. The force of the impact was so powerful he's lucky to be alive. If he does come out of his coma he'll be in a vegetative state, he'll be like a young child. The brain scan shows colossal damage, most of the bones in his face are shattered; his jaw is broken in at least seven different places. He was pretty much crushed to death only he didn't die. It's miraculous he's still alive. To be honest Mr Shand, and this is between you and me. it would be better if he hadn't survived. He wont be able to answer any questions. I doubt he'll remember anything about the crash, you might as well send your policeman home because Mr Ambrose isn't going anywhere.'

'Thank you, Mr Bolan but as he's still a suspect in a triple murder investigation the policeman stays on guard by his door.'

'As you wish, Mr Shand.'

Shand walks up to the policeman on guard.

'Constable?'

'Yes, Sir.'

'I want you to make records of everyone who comes and goes to see Mr Ambrose. Any family, friends, everyone understand?'

'Yes, Sir. Understood.'

'Plus I want to see these records every day, okay?'

'Yes, Sir, I'll make sure you get them everyday.'

Shand and Walker head for the car. Walker turns to Shand.

'Fancy a drink, Sir?'

Shand looks a bit astonished at Walker who has never suggested anything like this before. Shand checks his watch.

'Okay, Robert, why not? Where do you suggest?'

As they pull up outside the Celtic Knot, Shand says,

'Why? Do I know this place?'

'I've been here a couple of times to talk to the landlord, a Mr Ventura. This was the last place Adrian Jarvis was seen alive.'

'So why are we here?'

'I want to see his reaction when we walk in. He wasn't very helpful. All he wanted to do was chat up Miss Christi, the time she came with me.'

'I hope this is not some sort of persecution, Sergeant?'

Shand is smiling at his Sergeant.

'As if, Sir, I just fancy a pint, that's all.'

'As long as you're in the chair, Robert, fine with me. Let's go.'

As they enter the bar there are a few people sitting at the tables drinking. Shand and Walker wait at the end of the bar. As soon as Jenny, the barmaid, sees them she strolls towards them in a very provocative way.

'Good evening, gentlemen, what can I get you?'

Walker looks at her from top to toe and mutters to himself: 'What a knockout' 'I'll have two pints of your best bitter, please, and one for yourself?'

'That's very kind of you. I'll have a small glass of wine later.'

She puts the two beers down in front of them deliberately leaning over to show of her cleavage. That is what Harvey Ventura told her to do.

'There you are gentlemen. That'll be four pounds fifty, please?'

She gives Walker a big smile showing beautiful white immaculate teeth. As she walks away she looks back at Walker still smiling. He can't take his eyes off her. She has a stunning figure, slender and curvaceous. Shand takes his glass holding it up

'Cheers, Robert, I think you've pulled there.'

'You think so, Sir? She is a bit of a corker, don't you think?'

'Yes, Robert, I do. If I were a single man you'd have competition there.'

The clink of glasses signals the start of their evening. Jenny, at the other end of the bar is wiping glasses from the dishwasher. She is looking at Walker while she dries them. He cannot take his eyes off her. Shand looks around the bar, it is quite big. He believes it could hold around a hundred people at anyone time. At the opposite end there is a small stage with disco equipment waiting to be set up for a karaoke night. It is decorated in an old style to suit the setting with wooden beams on the ceiling, leadlight windows and rugs on the floor under the tables, old country paintings a hundred years old hang from the walls. One depicts a scene of a boy sitting on a horse pulling what looks like some sort of plough. It reminds Shand of John Constable's Flatford Mill. A smell of furniture polish hangs in the air. The beer is good, an old English ale strong and dry. Shand thinks to himself: 'you wouldn't need too many of these'

They are both enjoying the evening talking about all sorts of topics. For a moment they seem to forget about the case they are working on. Shand is about to order another two pints when Harvey Ventura appears behind the bar. He sees them standing at the end and asks Jenny who they are. He thinks he recognises one of them. But he's never seen the tall blond muscular one before.

'Who are those two at the end of the bar, Jenny?'

'No idea, I've never seen them in here before. The dark one is a bit tasty.'

'How long have they been here?'

'About an hour or so. Why?'

'No reason I just thought I recognised one of them that's all. I'll serve them this time, okay?'

'If you must. I think the dark one wants me to serve him. He keeps gazing at me.'

'He's all yours. I just want a chance to talk to them, that's all.'

Ventura walks down the bar looking at Shand and Walker. He can't recall where he has seen one of them before. It starts to worry him.

'Good evening, gentlemen. What can I get you?'

Shand holds up his glass.

'Two more of the same, please.'

He's pointing at Jenny.

'She knows what we're drinking.'

Ventura looks at Jenny indicating to get their drinks. He stays his side of the bar looking at them.

'So, gentlemen. I don't believe I've seen either of you in here before have I?'

He has the advantage of looking down at them because the bar floor is elevated his side. Shand can see he is using his extra height to intimidate them. He stares at Ventura with a gaze of authority pulling himself up straight to meet his glare.

'You must have a good memory with all the people you get in here.'

'Some I remember, some I don't. I'm sure I would remember you. What did you say your name was?'

'I didn't. What did you say your name is?'

Shand is getting the upper hand on Ventura because he is more used to asking questions than Ventura is. Ventura can see he is loosing his advantage. He leans on the bar to level himself with Shand. Jenny pushes in front with the two glasses of beer. Making sure they can see more of her cleavage this time, she winks at Walker who hands her a ten-pound note saying again.

'Don't forget to take one for yourself.'

'Are you trying to get me drunk?'

'Only if I can get drunk with you?'

Jenny shows her beautiful teeth again.

'That could be arranged if you'd like to.'

Walker acts on her proposition by saying to Shand.

'Do you mind if I go to the other end of the bar and talk to Jenny?'

'Not at all, Robert, I will stay here and have a chat with my new friend.'

Shand turns back to Ventura. They now have eye-to-eye contact.

'So, Landlord, tell me. What do I call you?'

'My names Harvey Ventura. I'm the owner of this establishment. And you?'

'Shand. Neal Shand. I'm pleased to meet you.'

Shand offers his hand. Ventura takes it, feeling a very strong, firm handshake. He tries to return it but Shand lets go before he can.

'A very nice pub you have here, Harvey. I may call you Harvey, may I?'

'Yes of course. All my friends call me Harvey. Please accept the next one on the house. I like to make my new customers feel welcome.'

'Please excuse me. I have other clients to attend to.'

'By all means, Harvey. You go ahead.'

Shand moves down the bar to join Walker.

'So, Robert, how's it going?'

'Very well actually. I have a date on her next night off.'

'Okay, Robert. Let's go,'

Walking back to their car Robert asks:

'Didn't you like it in there?'

'The pub's okay. But I'm not sure about the owner, a bit too friendly for my liking,'

'How do you mean, Sir?'

'Asking too many questions for a pub landlord. It made me feel a bit uncomfortable. And he kept asking about you.'

'He should have recognised me. I've been twice to talk to him. But he acted as if he has never seen me before.'

'That's what I thought too. Why didn't he say something?'

'I guess we'll never know, Sir.'

CHAPTER THIRTY-ONE

As Shand pulls up outside his house he sees Molly and Annabel in the garden. Molly is playing with Sherper. He stands by his car watching them for a moment.

Molly looks up and sees him standing there. She comes running to him.

'Hi, Dad. Had a good day?'

She gives him a hug that takes his breath away.

'So-so, precious. I just came back from a drink with Robert.'

'Yes, I can smell the beer on your breath. Phew it stinks.'

'Sorry, precious. I only had two beers but it was strong ale.'

He moves towards Annabel who is reading on a 'chaise longue' wearing a white sleeveless low neck t-shirt with an old pair of cut off jean shorts. Her long shapely legs are crossed displaying elegant thighs. His eyes move first up her flat stomach then to her breasts; her nipples stand prominent through her t-shirt. He cannot take his eyes off her. She looks up from her book revealing a stunning smile. She stands up and walks slowly and provocatively to him, she puts her arms around his shoulders. He feels her breasts against his chest. As she kisses him with desire he can feel himself becoming excited. She pulls away looking deep into his eyes.

'Welcome home, sweetheart.'

'That's what I call a welcome,' he says with longing in his mind,

'How was your day?'

'Infuriating, would be a good way to describe it. I'll tell you over dinner.'

Shand waits until Molly leaves to walk Sherper before he tells Annabel about his visit to the hospital to see Arthur Ambrose and what the doctor told him. She puts her hand up to her mouth in bewilderment.

'My God, that's dreadful. Poor man.'

'Don't feel too sorry for him. I think he's one of the people who are connected to the triple murders. Only I can't be sure. Plus, I would love to have another talk with Doctor Cole only the Chief, in all his wisdom, let him go and now he's disappeared. And we still have a missing person. But on the brighter side, Robert has found himself a girlfriend.'

'That's wonderful. Tell me who? He's such a charming man.'

'The barmaid from the Celtic Knot. Her name is Jenny. A lovely girl, very shall we say voluptuous.'

Annabel looks at Neal with a frown.

'You mean she has big breasts, and long legs?'

'Really, I can't say I noticed.'

She throws her napkin at Neal amused.

Molly returns from walking Sherper. Both are out of breath. Sherper heads straight for his water bowl lapping at if furiously. Molly looks red in her face. Shand looks at her concerned.

'Have you been running?'

'Yes, Sherper chased a cat. I had to keep up with him but don't worry. I'm not as fit as I thought I was, that's all. I'm going up for a shower. See you two later.'

Shand turns back to Annabel.

'Don't mention what I just told you to Molly.'

'Of course not, but I may use this in the paper and at the TV studio. It will make a great story, and it might help to find the other people your looking for. Who knows?'

'What do you mean? I don't understand.'

'When people read or watch this kind of thing it often makes them think about something they might have seen, and bring back memories that they had forgotten about. You never know what it will unravel.'

'Okay, it's up to you, but remember there are still three other murderers out there and one of them could be the individual who called you. Doctor Cole said he lent the number to a friend. We think that it could be Arthur Ambrose but I can't interview him. And from what the specialist told me I'll probably never get the chance.'

'So, where do you go from here?'

'To be perfectly honest, Annabel, I don't know. I'm stumped. I have three of the most stomach-turning murders I have ever seen. Furthermore I still have a person missing. I don't have a clue where to start looking. A suspect in hospital, whom I can't speak to; another suspect who disappeared, slipping mysteriously away. He could be anywhere.'

Annabel leans across the table taking Neal's hands in hers giving him an affectionate glance. He smiles back. Then she abruptly sits up staring into Neal's eyes with a look of someone who has just had a brilliant idea.

'I've just thought of something, or someone that might help.'

Neal, still bowled over Annabel's beauty, sits up in his chair, puts his wine glass on the table and leans closer to her.

'Go on, I'm listening.'

'Maybe Miss Collins can help find your missing person.'

'But she's a medium, she only talks to dead people, doesn't she?'

'No, not necessarily. She told me when we were at the castle she also feels when someone is in pain or suffering. If Daniel Winter has been missing for eight days and assuming he's still alive, she may be able to pick up on his torment. It's got to be worth a try. What do you think? You've got nothing to lose, have you?'

Neal leans across the table and plants a huge kiss on Annabel's forehead.

'I think you're not only the most beautiful woman I have ever met, you're also the smartest. I'll call the police station now and get them to bring her in tomorrow morning. Even though she gives me the creeps.'

Annabel sit back in her chair, pours another glass of wine, looking smug.

Miss Collins is waiting in the reception area at 9 a.m. as requested. When Shand arrives she is sitting bolt upright staring into space with a look of blankness about her. Shand greets her with a firm handshake.

'Good morning, Miss Collins. Thank you for coming this morning.'

'You're welcome, Mr Shand. How can I help?'

'Let's go upstairs to my office and I'll tell you why I called you in.'

He looks round smiling at her. He can't help thinking she's floating along the corridor behind him. She still wears the same full-length cloak that covers her feet. In his office, Shand invites her to sit and offers her a coffee, which she politely refuses. He sits opposite her and explains his problem. She glares into Shand's eyes with such intensity it makes him feel awkward. He finds himself tugging at his shirt collar.

'So, Miss Collins, that's about everything. Do you think you can help me in finding Daniel Winter?'

He feels she is burning into his eyes.

'I can try to make contact but I need more information about him first.'

'Tell me what you need? I'll try my best to give it to you.'

'It would help if I could go to his house and walk around to get a feel for him.'

'Okay, but I'll have to call his mother first to see if she approves. I have a picture of him, would that help while I call his mother?'

'As you wish, Mr Shand.'

She takes the photograph and caresses it.

Sergeant Walker enters the office and sees Miss Collins sitting there.

'Okay, Sir, Mrs Winter agrees. She's at home now and asked for you to come straight away.

As they enter Winter's house, Shand and Walker explain who Miss Collins is, and why they brought her here. Mrs Winter stares at both of them.

'It all sounds a bit strange to me. But if you think it will help.'

Shand tries to reassure her, telling her what happened at the castle.

CHAPTER THIRTY-TWO

Miss Collins is standing in Daniel Winter's bedroom, her eyes closed, she seems to be whispering something under her breath. She touches his bed, letting her hand feel it her fingers slowly stroking the duvet. She then moves to the wardrobe, opens the door, touching all his clothes, pulling a shirt to her nose, she inhales then exhales intensely. Gradually she walks to the dressing table, picks up various items and holds them to her face. She moves on to the bathroom looking for anything belonging to him. She picks up his comb pulling a few hairs from it holding them in her hand rolling them over and over raising her hand to her face and sniffing the hair. Finally she walks down the stairs slowly one at a time carefully gripping the banister, touching and patting it like an old friend. She enters the living room where Shand, Walker and Mrs Winter are drinking tea waiting for her to speak. She stops in the middle of the room with her concentrated look not saying a word. She turns to Shand.

'He's alive, but only just. You must find him today or it will be too late.'

Shand looks at Walker then at Mrs Winter and last at Miss

Collins his eyes wide open, mouth opening and shutting unable speak. Walker seeing Shand's state says:

'Miss Collins, do you have any idea where we should look?'

'I hear waves with an echo sound, as if it were somewhere inside. It's dark and cold there.'

'Could it be a cave?'

'Yes that's exactly what I think. It's a big cave with two entrances; one from the sea and another from the cliffs. The ground level seems higher than the sea and I can see steps carved in the rock. If a boat anchored there, people could climb up those steps into the cave and finally reach the top of the cliffs without being seen.'

Shand is absorbed in deep thought. His arms folded, one hand stroking his chin. He is staring at the threadbare carpet but his thoughts are elsewhere.

Suddenly and loudly he snaps his fingers.

'The smuggler's cave. It has to be. Miss Collins just described it perfectly.'

Both Shand and Walker are on their mobile phones running to their car, telling the police station to get the fire brigade and the paramedics to meet them at the smuggler's cave as quickly as possible. They take Miss Collins with them leaving Mrs Winter standing at the doorstep holding a tissue to her mouth.

As they came to Mrs Winter's house in an unmarked police car, Shand slams the flashing blue magnetic light on the roof. He flicks a switch on the dashboard which starts the sirens screaming, telling Walker to step on it.

The paramedics and the fire brigade arrive at the same time. The noise of their sirens and flashing blue and red lights frighten the sea gulls, who fly in circles above them squawking down at them as if they were disgusted at being woken up from their slumber. Shand and Walker pull up between the ambulance and the fire engine. They quickly explain where to search and who to look for. The fact Daniel Winter had been in the cave for nine days they must expect to find him in an extremely poor condition. The paramedics go in first, one of them holding a powerful torch to help their way safely over the rocky, uneven and slippery ground. The fire brigade follow closely behind carrying cutting equipment and more powerful torches, moving them in a sweeping motion to light up the cave.

Shand and Walker wait by the entrance to the cave with Miss Collins. Suddenly, one of the paramedics shouts:

'Over here.'

The other crews follow. They discover a body lying in a foetal position, which seems to be asleep. They see a heavy rusty chain attached to his ankle covered with blood. The paramedics franticly get to work on the body, the firemen on the chain.

Shand is pacing backwards and forwards outside the cave like an expectant father. Suddenly he sees the paramedics hurrying from the cave with a stretcher between them carrying it as carefully as possible over the slippery surface, one of them holding a saline drip as high as he can with one hand, while holding the stretcher with the other hand. Shand follows them to the ambulance.

'Is he still alive?'

'Barely. We need to get him to hospital as fast as possible.'

Shand lets them carry on with their work. The firemen appear from the cave, one of them holding the chain that kept Daniel Winter captive. Shand approaches him holding out his hand.

'Can I have that, please? It's the evidence that Winter was kidnapped.'

The fireman hands it to Shand. He holds it carefully feeling its weight.

'Is there anything else in there I should see?'

'Not really, Sir. The sea washed most of the rocks where we found him. There would be no use sending in forensics, they wouldn't find anything.'

Shand thanks them and returns to his car. They all drive off, leaving no evidence of their presence except tyre marks where they all stood.

Back at the police station, Shand and Walker go straight to their office with Miss Collins who accepts the offer of a coffee this time. She goes to sit in a chair opposite Shand's desk holding her mug in both hands blowing the steam away softly.

'Miss Collins, I'm extremely grateful for your help in this matter, it's been invaluable. You probably saved Daniel Winter's life.'

She takes a sip of her coffee unperturbed by the events of this morning. She gives Shand one of her stares. But this time a slight smile appears on her face.

'I feel and see things that you don't. That's all. It's a gift. I'm stuck with it so I try to use it to help people who can't see what I can.

'Well, anyway, Miss Collins, I am extremely happy you're here. Thank you. It was actually Miss Christi suggested I call you.'

Shand thinks he can still see that slight smile on her face as she raises her mug of coffee to her lips. When she has drunk her coffee he walks her to the main exit holding out his hand to shake hers. She takes it softly holding his hand in both of hers. Shand can feel a tingle running up his arm. Her face shows sadness and sorrow. She looks into his eyes again with intensity and longing that cuts deep into him.

'Find these people, Mr Shand. What they are doing isn't natural. Normal people don't treat other human beings this way.'

Her hands slip away from Shand's. She turns away from him and walks off. Shand stands by the door watching her.

CHAPTER THIRTY-THREE

St Mary's hospital is a hive of activity. Doctors, nurses and ward orderlies are running from ward to ward as if they were in a relay race with all kinds of medical equipment dangling and crashing from stainless steel trolleys. Intercom systems bellow out for assistance, individual beepers vibrate and flash in the breast pockets of their white coats beside their packets of cigarettes.

The intensive care ward is on the ground floor allowing easy and fast access to the paramedics arriving with their patients. By the coffee machine, Shand and Walker are waiting for the specialist to come and talk to them after he has completed his examination of Daniel Winter. Shand is pacing again, as he did when he was outside the smugglers cave. Walker is sitting reading a three-month-old edition of Woman's Weekly. The double doors keep swishing open with people coming and going. Each time Shand looks up to see if it is the doctor coming through. He checks his watch, every thirty seconds. Eventually he appears in the corridor heading for the coffee machine, pushing a coin in the slot selecting his drink. He looks at Shand while taking a sip of coffee.

'Are you the police officer in charge?'

'Yes I'm Detective Chief Inspector Shand. And this is Detective Sergeant Walker.'

The specialist holds out his hand in a greeting. Accepting it, he feels a strong firm grip. The doctor is a young man of about thirty years old, tall with a slim build. His face shows fatigue; he has dark rings around his eyes, and looks like someone who hasn't shaved for at least two days. His black hair is cut neat and short. His bronzed completion tells Shand he is not English, more like Spanish or Italian.

'Gentlemen, I'm Doctor Perez. Shall we go to my office? It will be easier to talk there.'

He gestures to Shand and Walker to follow him. His desk is cluttered with files waiting to be looked at. It is a small office with a

Venetian blind hanging at a slant in front of a high window, which lets in a glimmer of light illuminating the over filled filling cabinet leaning against the back wall, the top draw partially open with an overload of flies bulging out from it. The doctor indicates them to bring the two chairs closer to his desk that are against the far wall.

'So, the good news is your man is alive. He's in an exceedingly bad way; he's suffering from exposure, hypothermia, hunger and severe blood loss. He also has numerous cuts and abrasions around his head and face. He's lost several teeth because someone was beating him, what looks to me, like on a daily basis. He also has five broken ribs. His genitals are swollen to almost twice their normal size. I would hazard a guess he was kicked very hard and many times in the groin area. I'm particularly worried about his ankle where the manacle was cutting into him. The rust got inside his wound and might cause gangrene. If it does I'll have to consider amputation before it spreads. He's still unconscious. I have him on some pretty strong medication.'

'So when can we talk to him, doctor?'

'My advice is to come back in the morning, he should be coherent then but only for a few minutes. I don't want him distressed. I'm not sure he can talk because of the injuries to his mouth. If it hurts him too much I'll have to ask you to stop. Do you understand, gentlemen?'

'I'm going to put a police guard outside his room. He's a vital witness in a murder investigation.'

'I don't have a problem with that, Mr Shand, as long as he

doesn't get in the way.'

Leaving the hospital, Shand stops by the door looking back deep in thought.

'This is the best break we've had in this case, Robert. I hope our man comes round soon. Maybe he can identify the killers.'

'I hope so, Sir, this case has been going on far to long. We've been hitting brick walls at every turn. We need this break.'

Back at the police station, Shand's door opens quietly. He sees the Chief entering and coming to stand in front of his desk. Shand ignores him pretending to study his case files. A small cough signals Shand to look up.

'Morning, Sir. Lovely day, don't you think?'

The Chief can detect more sarcasm in Shand's voice.

'Mr Shand, I had rather hoped I would have heard of the recent events from you, and not from civilian staff, and corridor gossip. Nevertheless, I congratulate you on finding Daniel Winter. Good police work. Well done.'

Sitting in his chair Shand looks up at the Chief, giving no indication for him to sit.

'I can't take all the praise, Sir. Firstly it was Miss Christi who suggested I bring in Miss Collins and secondly it was due to Miss Collins gift, shall we say, that we found him. I just acted on the information given to me.'

'Yes. Police work has certainly changed since my days out on the beat.'

Shand has to stop himself sniggering at the thought of the

Chief out on the street giving out parking tickets and helping old ladies cross the road.

'I agree, Sir, but the fact is, nowadays we have to use every opening that presents itself to us. If it's effective then why not?'

'I agree, Mr Shand. Unquestionably. When will you be able to speak to Mr Winter? We need any and all information he can give us.'

'The doctor told me to come back tomorrow morning. He's been heavily sedated because of his injuries. I've also put a twenty-four hour police guard outside his room. I don't want anyone except hospital staff talking to him until I've had a chance to interview him. If this story gets into the papers, and I'm sure it will with Miss Christi involved, there could be trouble.'

'In what way do you mean?'

'Because, Sir, remember there are still three of this gang, or whatever these lunatics want to be called, loose out there. If they find out we have found Daniel Winter alive they will most probably try to get to him to stop him talking. It's highly feasible he can identify one, or maybe even all three of them. Now we are so close, I'm taking no chances with him. I'd sleep in his room myself if I had to. There's too much at stake here to be nonchalant about it.'

'Very well, Mr Shand, I'll leave it in your capable hands. But please, keep me informed as soon as he starts talking?'

Shand leans back in his chair, the leather groaning with his weight. He doesn't bother replying, he is just smiling at the Chief. He watches him clumsily make his way out of his office like a child who has just been told off.

Walker turns to Shand, not being sure if he should comment or not about how Shand greeted the Chief.

'I know what you're thinking, Robert. I'm not showing as much respect as I should to the Chief. But the fact remains, as far as I'm concerned, he's just a desk jockey nowadays. He doesn't have a clue what's going on out there on the street. His job is to handle numbers and to show-off to the police commision board what a good egg he is. He has lost sight of what real policing is all about. So I acknowledge and respect the rank he holds, but not the person who's holding it. Not this time anyway.'

Walker stays quiet, there's no need to reply, he agrees totally with Shand.

'How about a strong coffee, Sir? Maybe a little of my special milk?'

'Okay, Robert. But don't you have a date with the adorable Jenny tonight?'

'Yes, I'm picking her up in front of the Celtic Knot.'

Shand looks at his watch.

'You might as well leave now if you want to. We can't do much more tonight. At least we know where our man is.'

CHAPTER THIRTY-FOUR

As Walker approaches the Celtic Knot, Jenny is standing outside the door trying to pull it open. He parks his car and starts to walk towards her. She turns to him looking confused.

'Hi Jenny, nice of you to wait outside for me.'

'Oh, hello Robert, I can't open the door it's locked, I don't understand. I wanted to go inside to check the takings before the evening rush.'

'Do you have a key?'

'Yes, but only for the back door but I'm not sure if I should use it. Mr Ventura said only to use it in an emergency. He's very strict about that sort of thing.'

Walker stands back to look up at Ventura's apartment above to see if he can detect any movement but all the curtains are closed. He checks the front doors pushing and pulling at them, they seem locked and bolted. He can hear the bolts inside rattling.

'Is he supposed to be here this evening?'

'Yes, because I've got the night off he said this morning he would see me here before I went out with you. I was going to help him get the restaurant ready before I left. He has a birthday party of fifty people coming at seven tonight.'

Walker's mind starts racing thinking to himself: 'I wonder.'

'Jenny, stay here I'm going to my car to make a phone call, don't do anything till I get back okay?'

'Okay, if you say so.'

When Walker returns Jenny's standing smoking on the pavement.

'Okay, give me your keys I'm going to have a look inside. It's better if you stay here. I called my colleagues and when they arrive tell them where I am.'

Disappearing around the back of the building, he approaches the back door looking at the windows for any kind of life. He pushes the key slowly into the lock turning it gently. The door opens creaking and groaning from rusty hinges. He stands for a minute looking into a dark corridor and shouts:

'Hello, anyone here? It's the police.'

The only sound he hears comes from a grandfather clock in the bar. Its tick-tick seems eerie to him. He never noticed it before because when there are people in the bar and music playing, you do not hear it. He moves slowly down the hallway, gradually making his way to the bar. It is dark. And is difficult to see, his eyes not being adjusted yet. He waits for the bar to become clear to him. Everything looks normal. Tables, chairs and bar stools are all in place. The red standby light pulsating from the flat screen TV on the far wall, the microphone on its stand, up on the small stage for karaoke night are all in their usual place. He walks behind the bar, through the arch to the back room, which leads to the stairs of the apartment above. Standing at the bottom of the staircase, he shouts up.

'Hello anybody there? It's the Police.'

He waits for a reply but no sound comes back. Slowly he starts to climb the stairs looking up as he climbs, each board making a different creaking sound. Reaching the top he sees several doors. The first one leads to a bathroom. He has a quick look at it but all is clear. He moves along the landing looking into each room. Finally he reaches a big circular lounge with large bay windows and a wooden table at one end with the sitting area at the other side. A bookcase is fixed to the wall; it is full of books, pictures and ornaments, some souvenirs of holidays in the sun. On the coffee table there are a few magazines and two unopened letters. His eyes lock on the edition of today's local Gazette were the headline read *Local man held hostage for nine days found alive.*

    Hearing someone coming up the stairs, Walker's hand moves to his Arnold truncheon. He quickly extends it with a flick of the wrist clicking it into place and resting it on his shoulder as he was shown in the police training school. His other hand checks to make sure his handcuffs in their quick release pouch are ready for use. Standing behind the door holding his breath he feels a trickle of sweat on the nap of his neck running down slowly into his shirt. A silhouette appears by the door. Walker moves slowly, not breathing. As he appears from behind the door he sees a figure in the dark. It is tall with broad shoulders. Being too dark to see clearly who it is, Walker takes one last step; his mind is racing trying to remember what the training officer at the self-defence school told him to do in these scenarios. Beads of sweat are continuing to run down the side of his face. With a dry mouth, he shouts:

    'Police! Don't make any sudden or violent move or I'll strike!'

    Walker is in position with his left arm stretched out in front of him, and the right hand back over his shoulder with his baton ready. The figure' s arms slowly rise up as if in surrender he hears a familier voice speak.

'Robert. It's me, Shand!'

Both are standing not knowing what to do next. Walker moves his feet to get a more secure posture. He steps closer to the figure still with his baton at the ready. 'Turn round slowly.'

Shand keeps his arms raised high turning as he was told

'Robert, It's me. Put that thing away.'

Walker drops his baton arm and takes a step back.

'Jesus, Sir, you scared the shit out of me. I'm not used to this sort of thing. You can drop your arms now, if you wish.

'Thank you. They were beginning to ache. What are you doing here on your own? You should have waited for backup.'

'Sorry, Sir, I just thought I'd have a look. Jenny said it's very unusual for the pub to be closed this time of day. I didn't think about any danger.'

'Well, no harm done I suppose. What did you find?'

'Nothing, Sir. It all looks normal except there's no one here. One thing though, look at the front page of the Gazette.'

Shand picks up the paper reading the headlines aloud.

'If this has spooked our Mr Ventura then we need to find him and fast. Otherwise why would he run after seeing this?'

'You always had a bad feeling about him, didn't you, Sir?'

'Yes, Robert, it's like an itch I can't scratch. It's difficult to explain but now more than ever I want to find him. Let's get going.'

Jenny, still waiting in the street, is talking to a uniformed constable. Shand and Walker appear from the back of the pub. Shand speaks to one of the constables telling him to stay by the pub and report in if Ventura comes back. Walker stands beside Jenny.

'I'm sorry but something has come up. Can we do this some other time?'

'Okay. But what do I do now the pub's locked?'

'Go home. I'll call you later. Okay?'

Back at the police station Shand and Walker are franticly making phone calls to different departments making sure everyone is on the lookout for Harvey Ventura.

'I'm sorry, Robert, have I ruined your evening with Jenny?'

'No problem, Sir. This is more important. If Ventura is one of our killers I want to be there when we find him. Where do you think he would go?'

'I wish I knew the answer to that one, Robert. Unfortunately I don't have a clue. I just hope he doesn't vanish like Doctor Cole. At least we have Daniel Winter. I'm looking forward to talking to him in the morning.'

Shand looks at his watch stretching and yawning.

'We can't do any more tonight. Let's call it a day, what's left of it. Are you going to see Jenny?'

'Well, the night is still young, why not?'

'See you in the morning bright and early, okay?'

Walker looks at Shand smiling as he leaves the office.

'Night, Sir.'

Shand's mobile rings.

'Hello:'

A soft voice comes through the earpiece.

'The two women in your life were wondering if you were going to grace us with your presence tonight.'

He hears Sherper barking in the background.

'I'm on my way.'

CHAPTER THIRTY-FIVE

Harvey Ventura has been driving for hours and is now sitting in his car not knowing what to do. He reaches for his mobile phone, dials a number but after several rings he hangs up.

'Fuck it.'

He dials a second number. A voice answers.

'Hello.'

'It's me, can you talk?'

'Go on but be quick.'

'Have you seen the Gazette this morning?'

'No, why?'

'The fucking police have found Daniel Winter, that's why.'

There's a long silence and all Ventura can hear is breathing.

'So what the fuck are we going to do?'

'Where are you now?'

'That doesn't matter. We need to get together and sort this

out now.'

'Okay, okay, calm down, give me a moment to think. Is Winter conscious?'

'Apparently not but he's alive and that's all that matters, Sooner or later he will be conscious and then he'll start talking. Remember, he knows who we are.'

'Well, then we will have to pay him a visit in the hospital, wont we?'

'And how exactly do you propose to get past the police guard that is no doubt on guard outside his door?'

'We'll have to, wont we? If he comes round and starts talking, we're all in the shit.'

St Mary's is a hive of activity twenty-four hours a day. It's difficult to keep track of everyone coming and going. Ventura and the others enter the hospital unseen. Frank de Caux holding a bouquet of carnations tries to blend in with the surroundings as they approach the reception desk. Ventura spots a police officer talking to a pretty young nurse, his hand on the wall trying to lean close to her. He strokes her cheek with his fingers. There are doctors, nurses, paramedics and cleaning staff all going about their business. None of them take any particular notice of the three men looking at the information board.

'Okay, we're here. What now?' asks Clancy Belet.

'Let me think for a moment. First we need to find which room Winter is in, then we'll see. If that is the policeman guarding him then we might get lucky. He seems otherwise occupied with getting his hands on that little nurses tits. Let's hope she gives him the run-around for a while longer. The fucking little cock teaser,' replies Ventura.

'Calm down, will you. You've always had this bad attitude towards young women. He's only trying to chat her up, wouldn't you? A bit tasty if you ask me.'

'Ventura glares with such a look that sends a shiver down Belet's spine.

'No one is fucking asking you. We have a job to do; we're not here to ogle the nurses. Now, let's find Winter's room and get this over with.'

It takes them a long time to find the correct ward. A security guard watching them as they stand by a coffee machine starts to walk towards them.

'Good evening gentlemen, you look lost. Can I help?'

Ventura looks straight at him and smiles.

'Yes, we're here to see my friend's niece who's just given birth. We can't find the maternity ward. Could you help?'

The security guard stares at them suspiciously while checking his watch.

'It's a bit late for visiting, you'll have to come back in the morning.'

'Yes, we realise that. But you see, we had car trouble on the way down. Can't we just go for five minutes? It's been a long trip and we're tired. We have to travel back tonight to London and that's a long drive. I'm sure you understand, young man.'

The guard still not really convinced looks at the three of them. He hesitates but nevertheless gives in to their demand.

'Okay, it's the third floor. The lifts are over there. But you'll have to speak with the ward nurse on duty first. Most of the patients will be asleep by now.'

'Thank you very much, young man you've been most helpful.'

The security guard walks away, looking back at the three of them. He makes a note of the time.

'Okay, let's go. We'll have to take the lift or our little friend will get suspicious.'

The police officer sitting outside Daniel Winter's room tries to stay awake by drinking copious amounts of coffee. He is thinking:

'I hate night shifts especially as I have to sit here doing nothing'

The Doctors on duty make hourly calls on Daniel Winter. Each time they call they ask the police officer to look inside the room, where a mountain of medical apparatus are beeping and flashing, and a body lying very still on the bed with tubes coming out from his mouth and his arms.

'Poor bastard,' he whispers to himself.

Meanwhile Ventura and the others are trying to find Daniel Winter's room. One of them spots the policeman who suddenly had an emergency from drinking far too much coffee to try and keep awake is coming back from the toilet.

'Okay, we have to follow him. It has to be the one guarding Winter.'

'And then what? How are we going to get past a policeman?'

'One thing at a time. Let's just find the right room, then one of you will have to distract him while I'll go in and finish him off.'

'How are you going to do that?'

'The little fucker is practically dead already, it wont be difficult.'

They follow the police officer at a discreet distance. As soon as he sits outside the door, they move back from view where Ventura watches him reading his book.

'Okay, this has to be it, we can't wait any longer.'

The three of them devise a plan to distract the police officer guarding the room.

CHAPTER THIRTY-SIX

Opening the front door, Shand sees Annabel and Molly sitting in front of the TV.
Sherper is lying on the rug in front of them. Shand looks at his surroundings before he speaks.

'Good evening everybody.'

Both Annabel and Molly look up and smile. Sherper wagging his tail moves towards Shand who leans down to stroke Sherper on his head ruffling his ears.

'So you made it then?' asks Annabel.

'Yes, I'm sorry darling. It's been a long day.'

'Never mind, you're here now, that's all that matters. Sit down, I'll get you a drink.'

Shand sits down giving Molly a hug and kiss on her head.

'Hello sweetheart.'

She cuddles up to him not saying a word; the cosiness of being close is all she needs to feel loved. Before he knows it his chin is resting on his chest and he is softly snoring. Annabel brings in his drink looking at both of them resting in each other's arms. She puts his drink down on the coffee table, sits down to watch the news on the television.

Harvey Ventura stole a hospital cleaner's overall and equipment and is making his way to Daniel Winter's room. He spots the policeman on duty sitting reading his book.

'Evening officer, you're up late. Have you got someone special in there?'

The police officer looks up to Ventura a bit annoyed. He does not want to engage in conversation so late into the night. He attempts to ignore him trying to show interest in his reading. Ventura won't give up and keeps pestering the officer.

'So, who do you think will win the cup this year officer?'

He looks up slowly letting out a breath, irritated at the intrusion.

'I'm on duty. I can't talk right now.'

'Never mind. Can I go in and clean the room?'

'It's a bit late for that, isn't it?'

'No, not at all, we do this during the night because there're not so many people about. You know such as doctors and nurses running about all over the place.'

The police officer cannot see an identification badge on his overalls. He looks at Ventura doubtfully. He thinks to himself:

'Where have I seen you before?'

He knows he looks familiar but he cannot recall where.

'Let me see some identification, please.'

Ventura looks down at his overalls patting his pockets starting to sweat. He looks at the police officer grinning.

'I don't believe it, I must have left it back in the cleaning room. I'll go and get it, okay?'

The police officer stares at Ventura moving slowly closer to him. He has one hand on his nightstick discreetly undoing the small leather clasp ready to pull it from its holder. He keeps eye contact as his other hand moves to his personal radio pressing the red emergency call button.

'No, it's not okay. What's your name?'

Ventura starts panicking not sure what to do. He looks behind him hoping his colleagues will come to his rescue, but there is no one to be seen. He turns back to the police officer holding his hands up in the air by way of submission, smiling and sweating. For the first time in his life Ventura feels afraid and lonely, his fellow brothers having left him to face the policeman alone. The officer standing close to Ventura who can smell his breath, is looking down at his hands, the safety loop off from his night stick and his hand on the pommel ready to draw it, if necessary.

'I'll ask you again. What's your name?'

'It's err, Bob. Bob Smith. What's yours?'

Ventura tries to be friendly hoping the policeman will not push any harder.

The officer is very close to Ventura almost touching him.

'Okay, Bob Smith, let me see some sort of identification. As you seem to have forgotten your badge, how about your driving licence that will do?'

Once again Ventura starts to pat his pockets running his hands up and down his body, with both hands on his chest he looks straight into the officers eyes.

'I seem to have forgotten that as well, not my night, is it?'

'No, Mr Smith, it's not. Turn around and place your hands behind you.'

'Why? What have I done? Are you arresting me?'

'Yes, Mr Smith, that's exactly what I'm doing. Now do as I say.'

Ventura starts shaking at the thought of being arrested. He closes his eyes, takes a deep breath and brings his head down as hard and as fast as he can striking the officers nose with such power, he hears a sickening crunch as the nose breaks and blood gushes out. The policeman brings his hands up to his face shrieking as he falls to his knees. Ventura quickly pulls the night stick from the officers belt, raises it up slowly then brings it down on the back of the officers head with such a force he hears bones breaking. The officer falls to the floor and lies very still. Ventura moves quickly to Winter's door, opening it softly trying hard not to make any noise. He sees a body lying on a bed and all sorts of wires and tubes coming from him, machines beeping, red lights glowing in the dark, he moves closer to the body. He sees a figure lying motionless with only his chest moving in unison with the sound of the machine. He thinks to himself:

'If I turn the machine off that will do it. It's obviously keeping him alive.'

He moves fast to the back of the apparatus, finds what he is looking for and pulls hard. The lights go off and the body slowly stops breathing, just as he had hoped. He waits a moment looking at the body, making sure it is not breathing any more. For good measure he takes a pillow from under Winter's head, places it across his face and pushes down holding it as long as he dares before he makes his getaway. Once he is satisfied he opens the door. The police officer is lying on the ground motionless, there is a lot of blood around him. Walking fast then, running Ventura pulls off the overalls he stole earlier throwing them in a waist bin.

CHAPTER THIRTY-SEVEN

Shand wakes to the sound of his phone ringing. He fumbles for the receiver.

'Hello.'

A voice comes through urgent and assertive.

'D C I Shand, it's the police station. There's been an incident at the hospital you had better get down there straight away.'

Shand looks at his watch. 4.30 a.m. His head is fussy from the deep sleep.

'Okay, on my way.'

Moving quietly trying not to disturb Annabel who is sleeping, gently breathing her beautiful red hair covering her face.

As Shand approaches the hospital he notices more movement than usual for this time of the morning. Walking from his car he sees Doctor Perez who he talked with about Daniel Winter.

'Good morning, Doctor, I'm told there was a problem last night?'

'Morning, Mr Shand. I'm afraid the policemen guarding Daniel Winter has been attacked.'

'How is he Doctor?'

'Alive. But only just. He has severe head injuries and a badly broken nose.'

'And Daniel Winter?'

'I'm sorry, Mr Shand. Who ever attacked your policeman also switched off all the medical equipment, which were keeping Mr Winter alive. We got there too late. He's gone. I pronounced the time of death at 3.45 this morning.'

Shand still groggy from the deep sleep and being woken with all these problems cannot think straight.

'Come to my surgery, Mr Shand. We'll have some coffee.'

As Shand is sitting in Doctor Perez's office he sees all the files waiting to be looked at or tidied away. After walking in with two cups of coffee, Doctor Perez sits at his desk. He looks exhausted; the dark rings around his eyes are now black.

'So, Mr Shand, what's been going on in my hospital? I'm supposed to be healing people not finding them dead in their beds, as well as a policeman with his head half smashed in. This sort of thing doesn't look good. You know what I mean?

'Yes, Doctor, I do. I'm sorry this has happened. Mr Winter was a witness. He could have described one, or even two of the killers who were involved in these sickening murders we have had recently.'

'Yes, I've read all about that in the newspapers. Really gruesome stuff. Even I was sickened by what they did, and I've seen some pretty bizarre stuff in my time.'

'Yes, Doctor. I now hope that the police officer pulls through and he will be able to give me a description of the person who attacked him.'

'Well, I hope you don't want to talk to him anytime soon, Mr

Shand. He's not going to be speaking to anyone for a very long time. He's in a coma and I can't tell at present when or if he will come out of it he was hit with his own night stick those things are lethal in the wrong hands.'

Shand finishes his coffee and stands up.

'Okay, Doctor, thanks for the coffee. I'm afraid I'm going to have to take statements from everyone who was on duty last night. You do understand?'

'Of course, but I still have a hospital to run. I hope you also understand?'

Shand walks out into the corridor heading for the exit, with his mobile to his ear. The hospital is a mad house with people running to and fro. As Shand hangs up he sees Sergeant Walker coming through the main doors.

'Morning, Sergeant, I'm sorry to get you up so early but we've had an incident here and I need you to interview the staff on duty last night.'

'No problem, Sir. Whom shall I start with?'

'I believe there was a security guard here all night. See if he's still here and start with him. Then I guess the nurses.'

Sergeant Walker sets off in the direction of the security office leaving Shand standing alone looking at his phone thinking:

'I had better call the Chief. This will piss him off big time.'

After several rings he hears a groggy voice.

'Yes, who is this?'

'Morning Sir, it's DCI Shand. I'm at the hospital. There has been an incident here. I'm afraid our witness Mr Winter has been murdered, and the officer on guard duty has been severely injured. Sergeant Walker and I are interviewing the staff on duty last night.'

'All right, Mr Shand, thank you for keeping me informed. I'll make my way to the police station now. Is there anything I can do to help?'

'Yes, Sir, I'm going to need some more officers here to help with the interviewing process. Others will have to call the night duty staff who have left to their homes.'

'Very well, send a list of the staff to the police station and I'll get on with it. Keep me apprised with anything you find, please?'

As the phone goes dead, Shand finds himself standing in the reception area feeling a little lost. He looks up at the CCTV cameras, and says to himself:

'Are you on camera?'

The hospital is getting busier by the minute, phones ringing, people running backwards and forwards with all kinds of medical equipment. Sergeant Walker arrives looking at some notes.

'Do you have anything for me, Robert?'

'I think so, Sir. One of the security guards told me three men last night were acting suspicious. They asked him where the maternity ward was but then disappeared. As it was late he told them to come back in the morning.'

'Did he give a description of any of them?'

'Yes, but it's a bit vague I'm afraid. Average height, average build, that kind of thing. These people are not really trained to observe as we are.'

'I know, Robert, but did you see the CCTV cameras? We need to look at last night's film. We should do this at the station where we have the equipment.'

'Yes, Sir, I thought of that too. I have the DVD discs in my pocket. Let's go.'

After breakfast, Shand and Walker settle themselves in to watch the events of the night before. The first few hours give nothing of any interest. At about three a.m. they both see three men entering the hospital through the main doors, all three seem to be apprehensive, looking around as if they had never been inside a hospital before. Shand sits up and leans closer to the VDU.

'This looks interesting, Robert, get ready to freeze the picture when I tell you.'

Both watch the three men walking to the reception desk. Suddenly Sergeant Walker freezes the screen. Shand looks astonished.

'I didn't say freeze, did I?'

'No Sir, but I know one of these men, I've seen him before and so have you.'

Shand scrutinises the screen.

'My God, Robert, you're right, it's our charming landlord, Mr Ventura.'

CHAPTER THIRTY-EIGHT

Harvey Ventura is running from room to room in the upstairs apartment of the Celtic Knot. He is busy getting together as many of his possessions as he can before the police come for him. He knows it will not be long before they figure out who murdered Daniel Winter. The order of the Freohr is falling apart with Arthur Ambrose in a coma in hospital, Doctor Cole missing, Frank de Caux and Clancy Belet running away after the mess they left behind at the hospital. The police will not take kindly to one of their officers being so violently attacked. Ventura goes downstairs to his bar taking a few moments to reflect on the business he built up over ten years to a busy and profitable public house. He pours himself a large whisky, which he throws back down his throat in one gulp. He cannot stand the thought of someone one else taking over his pub. He enters the kitchen and turns on all the gas hobs. Opening the oven door he can smell the gas escaping. The hissing noise scares him. He grabs a box of large kitchen matches from a shelf, lights one and uses it to ignite the whole box. The 'whoosh' of all the lit matches nearly burns his face. He then throws the box at the oven. He runs down the back corridor, past he toilets out to the car park. Before he gets into his car he turns back to look at the kitchen window where he sees a flicker of orange light dancing as if there were a discotheque going on inside. All of a sudden there is an almighty 'boom' as the gas explodes. The noise seems to shake the whole building, windows shattering and flames pouring out as if trying to escape into the night. He can feel the ground beneath him shudder. Although he is mesmerised by the sight of his property going up in flames, he has to force himself to remember why he did it. He slips into the driver's seat and puts the keys into the ignition. Starting the engine he still cannot take his eyes off the fire, which is now a raging inferno. He can feel the heat through the windscreen of his car. Reversing away from the building, he gives it one last look before he turns into the night away to what he hopes will be a new life.

Shand, on the phone to the police station, tries to get a team together to go the Celtic Knot for Harvey Ventura, telling them to wait for him, as he is a violent person. He advises it would be better if they sent an armed unit as well. He will join them there as soon as he can. Putting the phone down, he addresses Sergeant Walker.

'Okay Robert, lets go. We can't do anything more here. I want to find Ventura. I've sent an armed unit to the Celtic Knot but told them to wait till we get there.

'Is this it then, Sir? Do you think we've solved this case at last?'

'I'm sure, Robert, it all makes sense. Now these people have given themselves away we've got them banged to rights. We just have to go and round them up a bit like in the old western films. We mustn't forget there are still two unaccounted for. I'm hoping Ventura will give us their names when we question him. But one thing is for sure, there won't be any more murders.'

As Shand and Walker approach the Celtic Knot, they see a sea of blue lights flashing. There are four fire engines with two ambulances and several police cars all parked at a safe distance from the building. As they get out of their car they cannot believe what they see. Shand's mouth drops open in astonishment when he sees what used to be the Celtic Knot pub now a ball of flames reaching into the night sky. The heat is so intense he cannot get anywhere near the building. The fire Chief walks over to speak to him.

'Evening, or should I say morning? It's a bit of a mess I'm afraid but I don't think there was anyone inside, not at this time of day anyway.'

Shand can't take his eyes of the flames. He has never seen such a fierce fire before. He turns to the Fire Chief.

'The owner, a Mr Harvey Ventura, was he inside?'

'I'm sorry, Mr Shand, but until we get this under control I'm not prepared to send any of my men inside. It's far too dangerous, the whole building could collapses at any moment. And don't forget there is a cellar as well. If it collapses we will have big problems.'

Walker is also lost for words and transfixed by the colossal sight in front of him. The noise and heat is overwhelming. He whispers in Shand's ear:

'Do you think he is inside, Sir?'

'The Fire Chief isn't sure. He won't send anyone inside because the building is unstable and could collapse at any moment.'

Shand feels his mobile phone vibrate in his pocket. He has to walk away to listen to the call, the noise being too powerful to hear normally.

'Hello, DCI Shand.'

'Neal, it's Annabel. What's happening?'

'It's a long story. We found the killers on the hospital CCTV. I'm at the Celtic Knot pub, which is a ball of flames, and I don't know if Harvey Ventura is inside or not. It's too dangerous to go in.'

'Why are you looking for him?'

'Because he was on the CCTV as bright as day. He has to be one of the people who has been committing these murders.'

'My God, I never did like the look of him. It always gave me the shivers the way he used to look at me.'

'Well, I wouldn't worry about that anymore. Even if he's not inside he's in big trouble and I will find him. I have to put a stop to this once and for all.'

'Okay darling, I'd better get down there, this is going to be a big story for me.'

'Bring some sandwiches, I'm starving and so is Robert.'

'Okay, you got it. I'll see you soon.'

Shand walks back towards the building where the flames seem to be dying down after the Fire service have been dowsing it, for what seems like hours.

Shand approaches Walker who is talking to the Fire Chief

'Anything for me, Sergeant?'

'Not yet Sir, the Fire Chief says it's still too hazardous to go inside.'

'How did this fire take hold so fast?'

The Fire Chief talking on his walkie-talkie turns to speak to Shand.

'It would seem, Mr Shand, this fire was started deliberately. One of my men was able to get into the building before it blew up. He went into the kitchen and found what looks like a box of large catering matches inside the oven, which was open. I think we are looking at arson here. Plus there were several gas canisters that were used for the beer pumps which all went up at the same time. This is why we have such a ferocious blaze.'

Shand thanks the Fire Chief and walks away to stand by his car with Sergeant Walker. They are both leaning against the side of his Beatle, while Walker is on his mobile.

'I've got everybody out looking for our Mr Ventura just in case he wasn't inside. We have a good description of him and his car. Let's hope we find him soon.'

'Thanks, Robert. Annabel is on her way down with some breakfast for us. She also wants to take some photos for the paper.'

'That's very kind of her, Sir, but I don't understand why does she bring you breakfast?'

'Because, Robert, I had to leave very early this morning after the phone call from the police station. I didn't have time to eat anything.'

'And Miss Christi knew this, did she?'

Shand looks at Walker smiling.

'You're the detective Robert, you work it out.'

Walker cannot stop grinning at Shand.

'Congratulations, Sir, you're a very lucky man. I'm envious.'

'I count my blessings everyday, Robert. I know I'm lucky. I

didn't deserve a second chance at happiness but I've been given one all the same.'

Annabel pulls up at the car park. As she gets out of her car she is holding a large bag. Even at this time of day she looks like a fashion model. Both Shand and Walker can't stop themselves staring at her as she walks toward them.

'Morning, you two. Breakfast. There are ham and cheese sandwiches and a flask of coffee. Be careful, it's hot.'

She takes her camera out of her bag and starts to snap away for her newspaper. Both men are following her with their eyes. Walker's jaw drops open but he quickly closes it.

'I'm sorry, Sir. I was staring.'

Shand just smiles at him.

'It's okay, Robert. How about passing me some coffee and a sandwich?'

The fire is under control. The Fire Chief is talking to some of his men when Shand and Walker move closer to him to hear what he's saying. As it is daylight now the fire does not seem so fierce.

'Are you going to send someone in to see if there are people inside?'

'I'm still not sure if the building is safe. The structure has suffered from the intense heat and I'm not happy about risking it. If there were people inside they won't need rescuing any longer. It's far too late for that.'

Harvey Ventura is driving. He is not sure which way to go, all he wants to do is get away from town as fast as he can. He turns on the radio for the news. He hears the hourly bulletin about a mysterious and unexplained fire at the local public house. No one knows if there were people inside. The Fire service will not enter due to fear of structural damage to the building. Ventura reflects to himself:

'Good, this gives me more time.'

He notices a sign for the M5 motorway heading north, so he steers toward it pushing his foot down hard on the accelerator.

CHAPTER THIRTY-NINE

Shand and Walker leave the scene after the fire to go to the police station. Annabel is busy taking pictures and talking to the Fire Chief, she does not notice them go.

Walker looks puzzled.

'Didn't you want to say good-bye, Sir?'

'Don't worry Robert, I know her well enough now. When she gets involved in her work the earth could stop spinning, and she wouldn't notice. She knows where to find me. Come on, we have a man to find, don't we?'

'Yes, Sir, and the sooner the better. I still can't believe this sort of thing goes on in our town. It's incredible to think we actually knew some of these criminals.'

'It does make you think, doesn't it? Do we really always know who we are talking to?'

As they pull up outside the police station, the Chief is parking his car. He looks at Shand's old VW Beetle.

'Morning, Mr. Shand, what a lovely car. I have never noticed it before. You must spend hours on it to keep it in such a perfect condition.'

'Thank you, Sir. Yes, it's a bit of a hobby of mine.'

'Come to my office would you? I want you to brief me about the fire this morning.'

'Give me ten minutes first. I have a couple of calls to make then I'll be with you.'

They all walk off to their offices. The Chief usually uses the rear entrance to avoid any press people that might be hanging around the front office.

Shand and Walker enter theirs.

'Put some coffee on, please Robert. I need a caffeine fix before I go the Chief's office. He's going to want to know every minute detail concerning this morning.'

Shand picks up his office phone to call the front desk.

'Sergeant, any news on my all point bulletin I put out earlier?'

'If you mean the one about our pub landlord, I'm afraid not. We have everyone looking for him and his car. He can't have got far.'

'All right, Sergeant, as soon as you get anything, let me know first, okay?'

Shand puts the receiver down just as Walker hands him a

247

mug of coffee.

'Thanks Robert. This should help keep me awake while I'm with the Chief.'

Harvey Ventura has been driving for many hours when he finally sees a sign for a service station. He looks at his fuel gauge, which shows the tank is nearly empty. Driving carefully trying not to attract attention to himself, he indicates to leave the motorway. After filling the tank and he pays cash over the counter; he does not want to use a credit card for fear of leaving a paper trail. He cannot help noticing the pretty young girl behind the till as he is paying. He stares at her chest with lustful eyes making her feel very uncomfortable. She pulls her zip up on her jacket and gives him his change rapidly.

'What time do you finish work, gorgeous?'

She tries to look away her face turning red. The shop manager noticing this comes over to stand by her side.

'Is everything okay, Cindy?'

'Yes, thank you. This customer is just leaving.'

Getting the hint Ventura winks at her and walks away. He mutters to himself:

'Fucking whore. I know what she needs.'

As he leaves the shop heading toward his car, he sees a policeman standing beside it checking the number plate while talking on his personal radio. He stops dead in his tracks.

'Fuck, what now?'

The policeman is writing something in his notebook.

As he approaches his car, the policeman looks up.

'Morning, Sir. Is this your car?'

'Morning, officer. No, it belongs to a friend of mine; I'm just using it while he's on holiday. Is there a problem?'

'Could you give me your friend's name?'

Ventura is becoming anxious not knowing what to answer. He becomes aware of another police officer approaching and who starts to speak to his colleague.

'I'll ask you again, sir. What is the name of the registered owner of this vehicle?'

'I don't really know him that well. All I know is his first name is George.'

'So you borrowed a car from someone who you only know by his first name?'

'Yes, I know it sounds strange, but I needed a car, mine broke down this morning.'

'And where are you heading to, Sir?'

'I'm going to visit an uncle up in London.'

'Where in London?'

'I can't remember the name of the street. All I know it's somewhere in the east end. When I get closer I'll call him to get the address.'

'And where have you come from?'

'Why all these question's officer? I haven't done anything wrong.'

249

'Just answer my questions, please sir.'

Ventura is becoming very agitated. He can feel his temperature rising. His face is going red, and his breathing is becoming erratic. The police officers seeing this stand back a couple of feet taking up the defensive position. One of them goes for his quick cuffs, the other one for his baton. The first officer talks louder now.

'Turn around and put your hands behind you. Don't make any sudden or violent moves or my colleague will strike.'

With a catlike movement, Ventura leaps at the police officer who falls onto the ground. Ventura throws himself on top of him pinning him with his legs and punching him in the face with force and as fast as a professional boxer. The other officer pulls his baton and strikes Ventura across his back as hard as he can, making him fall backward in pain. The officer then strikes a second time and sprays him with CS gas in his face. Ventura falls off to the ground clutching his ribs. Both police officers descend on him grappling his arms to put the quick cuffs on as fast as possible. They pull Ventura up to his feet securing the cuffs at his back. Shocked, sore and breathing heavy and fast the first officer manages to speak to caution him.

'You are under arrest for assaulting a police officer. You do not have to say anything but anything you do say will be taken down in writing and may be used as evidence in a court of law.' He then falls to his knees coughing up blood.

Ventura hears sirens waling in the distance and more police

cars approaching fast. He whispers to himself:

'Fuck it, I'm done for.'

The shop assistant standing by the shop door watches the scene.

'God, he was an awful person. No wonder they arrested him. Good riddance I say horrible man.'

Shand is sitting at the Chief's desk giving him a blow-by-blow account of this morning's incident when the desk phone rings. He picks it up, listens and hands it to Shand without saying a word.

'DCI Shand.'

He listens carefully nodding his head.

'Okay, thank you. I'm on my way.'

He hands the receiver back to the Chief.

'Before you go rushing off, Mr. Shand. Who was that?'

'The traffic police. They have just arrested someone who fits the description of Harvey Ventura at a motorway service station. By all accounts, he attacked one of the police officers injuring him quite severely. They're bringing him here and I want to be in the custody suite when he arrives. This is a major breakthrough, Sir. We now have one of these criminals I can actually talk to.'

'Very well, Mr. Shand, I'll leave you to it but don't forget please keep me updated.'

Spacing in the custody suite, looking at his watch every few seconds, Shand addresses the custody Sergeant.

'How much longer before they arrive, Bob?'

251

'A couple of minutes, Sir. Even so, you know you can't talk to him until the doctor has had a look at him first, don't you?'

'How long will that take?'

'It will take as long as it takes, Sir. While this person is in my custody, he will be treated by the book. You will have to be patient. When the doctor gives him the all clear I'll call you, okay?'

'I understand, Sergeant. You're the boss here I just want to see him when he arrives then I'll go to my office and await your call. Is that alright with you?'

'Perfectly, Sir. Just let me do my job then you can do yours.'

Shand is reading the notice board when he hears the doors open. Four police officers, two on either side, hold Ventura, who is still struggling as hard as he can, shouting and spitting at the officers.

'Let me go, you fucking bastards, I've done nothing wrong.'

They walk past Shand, who cannot resist saying:

'Morning, Mr Ventura. I'm looking forward to speaking with you later.'

Ventura looks at Shand with venom in his eyes.

'Who the fuck are you?'

Shand does not respond and walks away smiling and thinking:

'At last I have one of these butchers. I can't wait to talk to him.'

When he enters his office he cannot help punching the air as if his football team had just scored a goal.

'Yes, we have him, Robert. I've just seen him. It's definitely Ventura, no doubt about it. As soon as the doctor has seen him, he's all ours. I want you with me in the interview room. You're as much involved in this case as I am.'

He sits behind his desk smiling. Then he picks up the phone.

'Hello, darling, I may be late tonight. We have a very important person in custody. I don't want to say too much over the phone. I'll see you later.'

CHAPTER FORTY

After two hours the custody Sergeant calls Shand.

'Okay Sir, the doctor has given him the all clear. You can come down now.'

'Robert, come with me. We're going to interview Mr. Ventura at last.'

In the interview room, Shand, Walker and two uniformed officers are standing behind Harvey Ventura, who is still wearing handcuffs. He looks calmer now but is still very agitated breathing heavily and sweating profusely.

'Mr. Ventura, you have been arrested for assaulting a police officer. However, I want to talk to you about a much more serious matter.'

Harvey Ventura is sitting up straight he stares at Shand with

253

such intensity making him feels a little uneasy.

'I'll admit to the assault, but I'm not talking to you about anything else.'

Shand, not reacting carries on as if he had not heard him.

'There have been a series of ritual murders here over the last few months, and I'm sure you know more than you're prepared to say.'

'I don't know what you're talking about. I want to see my solicitor now. I'm not saying another word until he's here. You're trying to fit me up.'

'Very well, Mr. Ventura, it's your prerogative. We will call one for you, or do you have one of your own?'

'I have the best in town. He'll get me out of here in no time. Just because I punched a fucking copper you can't hold me for ever.'

In their office Shand asks Walker to find the security guard who was on duty and the police officer that was attacked the night Daniel Winter was murdered.

'Show the officer the photo of Ventura because we need a positive ID. He'll have a hard time explaining why he was in the hospital at such an early hour of the day. Also try to get descriptions of the other two that were with him.'

Shand looks at his watch. It is still early so he calls Annabel.

'Hi darling, how are you?'

'Okay thanks. I have some lovely shots of the burnt-out pub. I also talked to the Fire Chief he said there was no one inside. The building was empty. And you?'

'I'm okay. I have a prisoner here that I'm sure can shed some light on the ritual killings, but he's going to be a tough nut to crack.'

'Do you have a story for me?'

'Not yet, it's too early to say, but I'm not letting this one go anywhere until I'm happy. I have Robert out getting evidence from the incident in the hospital. That should help but until then there's not much I can do.'

'You could come home and keep me company. Maybe I can think about other ways to relax you?'

'That sounds really inviting. Normally I would be there in a flash, but I have to wait here until Robert comes back. However, keep that thought in your pretty head.'

As soon as he hangs up the phone, it rings startling him a little.

'DCI Shand.'

'It's the custody Sergeant. Mr. Ventura's solicitor is here he wants to talk to you.'

'I'm on my way, Bob. Put him in an interview room, please?'

Mr. Remington-Smyth is sitting in the interview room looking through his notes. He is an elegant man of sixty years old and the family solicitor for thirty-five years for the Ventura family. As Shand enters the room Mr. Remington-Smyth extends his hand in a gesture of greeting. Shand takes his hand and smiles.

'Morning, Mr. Remington-Smyth. It's good of you to come

at such short notice.'

'Not at all, Mr. Shand. When I heard the Ventura name mentioned I rearranged my appointments for the day. They are old and valued clients of mine. Mr. Ventura Senior is a very close and personal friend of mine. A successful businessman. Do you know him?'

Shand wonders if he is trying to intimidate him. He therefore does not respond in any way. Staying neutral he sits gesturing Mr. Remington-Smyth to do the same.

'Mr. Ventura was arrested this morning for a serious assault on a police officer. However, I want to interview him about another very serious matter.'

'And what might that be, Mr. Shand?'

'I am sure you know we have had a series of sickening ritual killings of local people, some of whom were not exactly pillars of the community. None the less, they still didn't deserve to have their lives taken away in such a macabre way.'

'I read the newspapers, Mr. Shand. Even so, why does this involve my client?'

'Because I have reason to believe that Mr. Ventura is one of the men who were committing the killings, along with Doctor Cole, who has disappeared. And I also believe the local butcher Mr. Arthur Ambrose was equally involved. At present he is in the hospital in a coma, so I'm unable to speak to him. There are two more who are still at large that I'm anxious to find.'

'What evidence do you have to substantiate this?'

'I have my Sergeant interviewing the police officer who was attacked while guarding Daniel Winter. And a security guard who we believe can put Mr. Ventura at the scene.'

'So until you have this evidence, the only offence my client is charged with is assaulting a police officer. Is that correct, Mr. Shand?'

'For the moment, yes.'

'Then I must insist you release him. He's admitted to the assault. He claims the traffic officers intimidated him. He's willing to come to the police station once a day to report in. So I don't see the need to keep him here, do you?'

'I'm afraid I disagree, Mr. Remington-Smyth. I firmly believe he is one of these five men who have been executing local people. If I let him walk out of here I'm sure he will abscond. Why do you think he was at a service station early this morning? You do know his pub was burnt into the ground earlier today don't you?'

'Yes he told me. Even so, I fail to see the connection.'

'He was fleeing, trying to escape. The fire chief's report proves the fire was started intentionally. He also told the police the car he was driving was not his. We checked. It is his car, so why was he lying? For these reasons alone I'm keeping Mr. Ventura here. If I have to I will involve the Cabinet Minister, who has taken an interest in this case. A Lord Huxley, do you know him?'

'Are you threatening me, Mr. Shand?'

'Not at all, no. I'm trying to impress on you the seriousness of this case. If it turns out Mr. Ventura was not involved, I will apologise to him personally.'

'Very well, Mr. Shand. You can keep him for thirty-six hours. If by that time you have no new evidence he walks out of here, understood?'

'Absolutely, Mr Remington-Smyth.'

In his office Shand heads straight for the coffee percolator. The Chief appears beside him.

'Coffee, Sir?'

'No thank you, Mr. Shand, I have my own blend in my office. This stuff you drink looks dreadful. Tell me, how did it go with Mr. Remington-Smyth? I have never met him, but his reputation precedes him.'

'I can keep Ventura for thirty-six hours. If I have nothing more substantial he walks.'

CHAPTER FORTY-ONE

Shand is pacing again looking at his watch every couple of seconds.

'Where is Walker?'

When the phone rings he almost drops the receiver in his rush to pick it up.

'Shand.'

'Sir, it's Walker. I have good news. I thought you would want to know straight away.'

'Yes Robert, tell me what did you find out?'

'Okay, the police officer has regained consciousness and made a positive identification when I showed him the picture of Ventura. He couldn't tell me who the other two were. Also the security guard has identified Ventura as one of the three men at the hospital the night Daniel Winter was murdered.'

'Excellent work, Robert. We have him. Get back here as quick as possible we have a murder suspect to interview.'

Shand replaces the receiver. He contemplates calling the Chief with the news. 'I want to see the look on his face when I tell him.'

Shand knocks firmly on the Chief's door.

'Come.'

As he opens the door he can't help smiling. He feels all his Christmases have come at once. When he closes the door gently he sees another person sitting at the Chief's desk. He is taken aback momentarily.

'Come in Mr Shand. I don't think you've met Mr Brodie have you?'

'No Sir. I haven't had the pleasure.'

'Mr Brodie is a peer of the realm. He also sits on the board of Chief police Constables. You can speak freely in front of him. So what have you got to tell me?'

'Well Sir, Sergeant Walker is on his way back from the hospital with statements from the police officer that was attacked, and from the security guard that was on duty the night Daniel Winter was murdered. These statements positively put Harvey Ventura at the scene. I'm now confident he's one of the five people involved in the ritual killings. And as soon as Sergeant Walker returns I intend to interview Ventura and put this new evidence to him.'

'I'm impressed, Mr Shand. Outstanding police work. I will await your report.'

Shand smiles at the Chief and at Mr Brodie who has no particular expression on his face. As he walks back to his office he is thinking hard.

'I know this Brodie person from somewhere.'

It is irritating him because he cannot place him anywhere in particular. He sees Walker walking along the corridor.

'Robert, let me buy you lunch. We can't interview Ventura until he has had his lunch. So let's get out of here for a while?'

'You buying, Sir?'

'Absolutely, Robert. You deserve it after what you've discovered this morning.'

They are having lunch at the local Chinese restaurant and Shand cannot stop smiling.

'Why so happy, Sir?

'The evidence you have, Robert. This could mean the end of the case once and for all. We have Ventura. All we need for him is give us the names of the others and it's over.'

'I get the feeling, Sir, it isn't going to be that easy.'

'I agree. Ventura is a tough one for sure. But he won't go down for four murders, one attempted murder and several assaults all alone. I'm positive he will give us the rest of this gang of lunatics.'

'The thing that worries me, Sir, is the way the killings were carried out.'

'How do you mean, Robert?'

'These people are not your normal killers. What I mean is when they killed, it was in a ritual way as if they had some sort of code of conduct to go by.'

'A killer is a killer, Robert ,no matter how they do it.'

'I just think he won't talk. I believe he thinks he's living by some sort of code of conduct, and he will go to prison with some weird sort of loyalty to whoever ordered the killings.'

'You think there is a hierarchy involved here, Robert?'

'Yes Sir, I do. Remember Miss Collins talked about five men dressed in blood red robes with ceremonial daggers. This is not the work of one man. These people must have a big Chief somewhere ordering them.'

'This is exactly what I'm hoping Ventura will give us. Come on Robert, we have a long afternoon ahead of us.'

When they both enter the interview room, Ventura is sitting at the table with Mr Remington-Smyth and a uniformed police officer standing behind Ventura who is still handcuffed for security. Once Shand has finished with the preliminaries he looks straight at Ventura.

'Mr Ventura new evidence has come to light positively placing you and two others at St Mary's hospital the night Daniel Winter was murdered.'

Ventura shows no emotion.

'I also want to speak to you about the ritual killings that have been taking place here over the last few months. I believe you can help me with this.'

Ventura looks at Mr Remington Smyth.

'Mr Ventura, your solicitor is here as an advisor not to answer questions for you. Do you understand?'

The way he stares at Shand sends a shiver down his spine. His eyes are piercing into his soul. Nevertheless he keeps eyes contact trying hard not to let Ventura see that he is actually disturbed by his stare. Ventura leans forward resting his arms on the table, the handcuffs making a rasping sound as they hit the metal top. The police officer moves forward a step. Ventura takes a deep breath, closes his eyes and turns his head up to the ceiling. Exhaling he returns his stare to Shand a grin appearing on his face.

'I am but a very small cog in a very big wheel. You might have me but you won't ever stop us from doing our work.'

Shand is shocked at the calmness of Ventura and for a moment he is lost for words. He straightens up; he looks at Sergeant Walker then back to Ventura.

'And what exactly is your work, Mr Ventura?'

'To rid our community of these evil, disgusting and revolting pigs that walk our streets because you idiots don't have the fucking balls to do anything about them.'

Shand has never been so ruthlessly tested before. Once again he feels strange in Ventura's company, but he has to keep control of the situation.

'Are you telling me Mr Ventura that you were directly involved with all three of the ritual killings and the murder of Daniel Winter?'

Remington-Smyth leans forward pointing a finger at Shand.

'That's coercion, Mr Shand?'

'No, Mr Remington-Smyth, that was a direct question. You will be able to listen to it when we hear the tape of this interview. Now please, do not interfere with my questioning the suspect any more.'

Shand looks straight into Ventura's eyes. He is becoming more confident with his questions he knows he has him after what he just said.

'Shall I repeat my question, Mr Ventura?'

The room goes deadly quiet. It is as if everyone is holding their breath. Ventura eventually opens his eyes and speaks.

'Yes, I was involved and I'm proud of what I did. I will do it again if given the opportunity. I hope my victims suffered and are still suffering in hell.'

Shand sits back, not believing what he has just heard. He looks at his watch.

'I'm stopping this interview. We will resume tomorrow morning.'

He leans forward to switch off the tape. His face is close to Ventura's who is grinning at him.

Back in his office Shand is pouring a coffee. Sergeant Walker walks in holding the tapes of the interview. Shand holds the percolator in a gesture.

'Yes please, Sir. Although after this interview something stronger would be more appropriate, don't you think?'

'Yes Robert, I do, but for the moment we need to keep our heads clear. That was one hell of an interview. I've never had one like that before. I don't mind admitting Harvey Ventura scared me. God only knows how his victims must have felt.'

'He certainly is intimidating, I'll give you that much, Sir.'

'Okay Robert, I'm going to brief the Chief, then I think we should call it a day. So go home, or go and spent time with your new girlfriend what's her name?'

'Jenny, Sir. Remember she worked in the Celtic Knot. Should I tell her about Ventura?'

'No, Robert, don't say a word and if she asks try to avoid the question, okay?'

'Understood Sir. See you in the morning.'

Shand spends an hour explaining the interview and Mr Remington Smyth's interruption to the Chief who seemed unperturbed. He wished him luck for the following interviews with Harvey Ventura.

Shand climbs into his Beetle and heads for home feeling completely worn out. When he reaches the front door it opens swiftly by Annabel who welcomes him with a glass of wine in each hand. He smiles broadly at her slipping his are around her waist pulling her close to him he finishes his drink in one long swallow:

'Wow, she just gets more beautiful every day, he thinks to himself.'

The fact she is wearing a very short and see through negligee makes the greeting all the more inviting.

'Another one? You look like you need it.'

'Thanks, yes, it's been a hell of a day. The case is coming to a close.'

'Come and tell me all about it while I prepare dinner.'

'Did you cook dinner in that?'

Shand is pointing to Annabel's clothing.

'Of course not.'

'This is your desert, she does a twirl for him.'

She moves close pressing her body against his. He can feel her breasts against his chest. She kisses him long and hard then pulls away looking into his eyes with the look of hunger. Not for food but for love making.

Over dinner Shand tells her as much as he can. He doesn't want to jeopardise the investigation by saying too much. Annabel is listening and attentive.

'My God, its unbelievable, these people really think they're helping the community?'

'Yes, Annabel, the way he spoke today. I really think he believes he's helping in some very weird and macabre way. But I still need him to give me the names of the others. We're pretty sure Doctor Cole and Arthur Ambrose are two of them. But that still leaves two unaccounted for.'

Annabel puts her hands on his shoulders and starts to massage him gently.

'What you need is a distraction.'

She sits on his lap letting her negligee fall open displaying her firm breasts. Neal takes one breast in his hand and starts to kiss a nipple. She throws her head back in pleasure giving a soft sigh, which tells him he is arousing her. She takes his face in her hands kissing him with such vivaciousness he can hardly breath. She whispers in his ear:

'The living room, now.'

Holding her in his arms he moves to the carpet. She is smiling up at him with her arms around his shoulders. He lets her drop gently, sliding down his body touching her as she slips gradually to the carpet. She is lying there looking inviting. The top of the negligee having come off he can see her wearing a very skimpy pair of French knickers, her red pubic hair showing through them. She looks up at him.

'Aren't you a little over dressed?'

He undresses hastily showing his erection. Annabel holding open both arms lowers him onto her. He feels his penis slipping into her. She groans with pleasure biting his ear and whispering:

'Slowly darling, we have all night.'

CHAPTER FORTY-TWO

Next morning Shand is ready early; he wants to make a day of it. He is eager to bring this investigation to a close. He is eating hot buttered toast and drinking tea in the kitchen when Annabel takes his toast from him and eats it. With just a bath towel wrapped around her he cannot help thinking back of last night. He feels he would like to make love to her again, right here in the kitchen. All he would have to do is pull off the towel and she would be naked. He knows she would not object, she would agree to his wishes. He has to shake his head and try to remember why he got up so early.

'It's going to be a long day darling. I will try to get home at a reasonable time. Maybe we could do something tonight?'

'We did that last night remember? But if you're ready for a repeat performance it's fine with me.'

As she walks out of the kitchen she stops and slowly pulls at her bath towel letting it drop to the floor showing her full magnificence.

'Just in case you need reminding what your leaving behind this morning.'

The drive to the police station seemed so quick. Shand cannot shake off the picture in his head of Annabel standing in the doorway of the kitchen naked.

Still thinking, he walks into his office. Sergeant Walker is already at his desk shifting through paperwork.

'Morning Robert. Nice to see you here so early. Are you ready?'

'Yes Sir. I stopped in at custody on my way here. Mr Ventura had a peaceful night and is eating a hearty breakfast according the custody Sergeant. We can see him now if you wish?'

'Yes Robert, I do wish. I want to get started as soon as I've had a quick word with the Chief. Is he here yet?'

'Not sure, Sir, shall I give him a ring?'

'No, don't bother, I'll knock on his door. If he's not there we'll start with Ventura and I'll update him later.'

As Shand approaches the Chief's door he sees it is partially open. He can hear voices. Moving his head closer trying to listen he can hear two men speaking softly. One of them he is sure is the Chief, the other he cannot make out. He can hear parts of the conversation as he almost presses his head against the door holding his breath.

'If Ventura gives up the names of the other two, how will that affect us?'

'As far as I'm concerned it won't make any difference. There are many more brothers out there waiting to be called.'

'Maybe we should put a stop to this. We have been successful so far, we shouldn't push our luck. What do you think?'

'It's not our decision. We do as we are told.'

Shand is frozen to the spot. He can't believe what he has heard. Just as he wants to leave one of the Chief's secretaries walks past him.

'Morning Mr Shand. Lovely day isn't it?'

The Chief suddenly opens the door looking furious at Shand.

'Mr Shand, how long have you been standing there?'

'I've just got here Sir. I wanted to update you on Mr Ventura.'

'Come back later. I'm very busy this morning and don't want to be disturbed.'

The door slams shut with a loud thud. Shand is holding his hand up as if to knock he thinks better of it and drops his arm and walks back to his office. He enters and sits down at his desk taking deep breaths to calm himself.

'Everything okay, Sir?'

He's not sure if he should tell Walker what he just overheard.

'It's nothing, Robert. Let's get started with Ventura, shall we?'

Harvey Ventura is sitting at the table with Mr Remington-Smyth beside him with a different police officer standing behind him. Shand and Walker take a seat opposite Ventura. Shand leaning over puts a new tape in the recorder and presses the red record button. The tape makes its usual sound telling them they can start the interview.

'It's Friday the 10th. The time is 09.00. Present is DCI Shand.'

The others present in the room introduce themselves.

'Now Mr Ventura, you admitted yesterday being one of the people who have been committing these ritual murders. We know there are at least four others, Are you prepared to give me their names?'

Ventura leans forward to speak to Shand.

'What's in it for me if I do give them to you?'

'Nothing Mr Ventura. We don't do deals. It's your obligation to tell me.'

Ventura leans back in his chair, letting out a deep breath.

'Well you know about the good Doctor Cole. And then there's Arthur Ambrose. But you can't do anything with him, can you?'

'Thank you Mr Ventura. Yes, we had our suspicions about these two you have just now confirmed for me. What about the other two?'

'What other two?'

'We know there were five of you. We can account for three. That leaves two unaccounted for, doesn't it Mr Ventura? You can tell me who they are, can't you?' And also, did you have some sort of Chief giving you orders of who to kidnap and murder? I don't believe you did this on your own.'

'Are you calling me stupid?'

'Not at all Mr Ventura, no. But this sort of thing takes a great deal of planning and thought. Plus you all had other jobs and businesses to run, didn't you?'

'I've giving you two names. I'm not giving anymore. You'll

have to find out yourself who they are.'

'So you admit there are two others out there probably running scared, don't you think?'

'I really don't give a fuck. You do your job and leave me alone I want a cup of tea. It's my right, isn't it?'

'Absolutely Mr Ventura. But I just have one last question before we break for refreshment, would you mind?'

'Make it quick.'

'On each body we found a small statue of one of the three wise monkeys. Would you please tell me the significance of this?'

Ventura leans forward breathing hard, his eyes bloodshot and showing his teeth as if in anger, veins pumping on his neck.

'See no evil. Speak no evil. Hear no evil. These things the fucking bastards did not show their victims, did they? Mister high and fucking mighty policeman.'

'You kidnapped and murdered a fourth person, Mr Daniel Winter. Why?'

'Like I told the others, read your fucking Japanese history. Now I want a cup of tea and a cigarette. I'm saying no more.'

'Very well. Interview stopped at precisely 09.50 the same day.'

Shand stands up and walks straight out not making eye contact with Ventura and heading for the coffee machine pouring one for him and Walker.

'I don't think we're going to get much more from him. Robert. He has a very low threshold. No wonder he's so violent.'

'I agree Sir. But do we have enough to convict him?'

'Yes, I don't think we'll have a problem there. I would love to know who the other two are. It's so frustrating getting this close and still not having all of them. Why is he being so stubborn?'

'I wish I knew Sir?'

CHAPTER FORTY-THREE

Harvey Ventura and Remington-Smyth are drinking tea.

'Mr Ventura, I would urge you to give the police the names of the other two accomplices, it might help when the court considers your sentence.'

'No way, they stay free. Our work is not finished, there are lots more out there that will attract our attention, and will suffer as a result of it.'

'So, you're prepared to go to prison for the rest of your life knowing these people are walking free?'

'It's not just about me, it's about justice for the innocent. These people are murderers and rapists. We exacted our own justice because the police are too fucking scared to.'

'Why in such a inhumane manner?'

'To send a message to any others who might think they can get away with flaunting the law. No one escapes our law.'

'You're a courageous man, Mr Ventura. But you know you

will never be realised from prison, don't you?'

'I served my master well. He will make sure my time inside will be easy.'

'As you wish, Mr Ventura. If you refuse to cooperate with the police or me then there's nothing more I can do for you. I've given you my advice, it's up to you.'

With those last words, Mr Remington-Smyth stands up and knocks on the door, a police officer opens it to let him out.

Shand is at his desk when the phone rings. He picks up the receiver not looking at it, his eyes still scrutinising the paperwork in front of him.

'DCI Shand.'

'Chief Inspector Shand. It's Mr Remington-Smyth. Can I come and see you?'

'Of course, I'm in my office all day. Please come when you're ready.'

'One hour then.'

Shand replaces the phone not taking his eyes off the paperwork. Sergeant Walker spins round in his chair to face Shand.

'Sir, I was thinking, would you like to come out for dinner one evening with Jenny and I? We've been talking about it for a while and she wants to meet you and Miss Christi, of course.'

'Thank you Robert, I would really enjoy that. Your place or mine?'

'I was thinking of the new Indian in the high street. My

treat.'

'Perfect, we both love Indian food. I'll speak to Annabel and get back to you, but we go dutch okay?'you're just a poor seargent, I remember those days well.

Before Walker can answer the door opens. The Chief is standing there looking very worried.

'Sergeant Walker, would you give us a moment please?'

'Of course Sir, no problem.'

'Good chap, close the door behind you.'

The Chief sits in front of Shand, resting his hands on his knees.

'Mr Shand, I'm very worried about what you might have overheard yesterday while you were waiting outside my office. Please be truthful with me?'

'Very well, Sir. I heard you talking to someone, I don't know whom, but you were talking about Harvey Ventura. Something about 'Brothers' if I'm not mistaken. It was a bit muffled. I couldn't hear everything that was said.'

'Hmm, just as I thought. You see, Mr Shand, I was actually having two conversations at the same time. One was about Mr Ventura and the other about my Lodge, if you know what I mean?'

'I think so, Sir. If that's the case then its not really any of my business is it?'

'No, Mr Shand, its not. But please don't misconstrue that there was anything more than just an innocent conversation with a friend.'

'Very well, Sir. But there is one thing that worries me.'

'What might that be, Mr Shand?'

'If it was an innocent conversation with a friend, then why were you talking about Harvey Ventura? He is a major part of this investigation, which is still at a very delicate stage?'

'The person to whom I was conferring with is a Chief Constable from another force. He was showing great interest in this case. Does that answer your question?'

'As I don't know who it was, then I'll have to take your word for it, won't I?'

'Yes Mr Shand, you will. Please don't forget who's in charge here. I'm not used to my staff questioning me. Do I make myself clear, Mr Shand?'

'Crystal clear, Sir. Now if you don't mind I have a mountain of paperwork to clear before I go home tonight.'

Shand watches the Chief leave slowly hesitating by the door as if he were going to speak, but he walks off turning his head and nodding.

Shand returns his attention to the paperwork that seems to be swallowing him up. Sergeant Walker reappears holding more files. Shand looking at his watch closes his computer and then switches off every light in the room.

'Come Robert. All this will still be here in the morning. The first pint is on me.'

The morning newspapers headlines read: 'Bank Manager and School

Head Master resign from their posts with immediate effect.'

Shand is in the kitchen reading while eating breakfast when Annabel walks in.

'Look at this. Did you write this story?'

'No, I didn't cover this one, why?'

'It's a bit odd, don't you think? Two leading men in the community, both quitting at the same time.'

'Can't say I'm that bothered. I'm too old for school and I don't bank with this branch. But I guess it does look funny.'

Shand looks at her. She is wearing two bath towels, one around her body and the other on her head.

'Are you going to drop the towel again?'

'Sure, which one?'

'Both.'

'That's a bit greedy of you, Mr Policeman. If I do, you will have to do a thorough investigation of what's underneath, wont you?'

'That could take some time, and I have to be at the station in half an hour.'

'Pity. I'm working from home today, so I can stay like this if you want?'

'Better not, you'll catch your death in those damp towels. But a small peak before I leave would keep me going for the rest of the day.'

Annabel smiles as she takes off the head towel. Shaking her head, her beautiful red curls drop to her shoulders.

'Is that it?'

Her smile gets more passionate as she starts pulling very slowly at the knot holding the other towel up. She pulls her right arm away from the towel and it drops to the floor. Totally naked, she moves towards Neal pressing herself against him. Her mouth eagerly searches his lips kissing him with such passion he has to gasp for breath.

'If there's anything I can do for you, you know where to find me.'

Neal watches her perfectly formed buttock cheeks move in unsion as she walks away.

CHAPTER FORTY-FOUR

Shand is the first one in the office. The pile of paperwork is still sitting on his desk. He is standing by the coffee machine waiting for it to finish boiling when Sergeant Walker arrives whistling a tune.

'You seem happy this morning, Robert?'

'Yes Sir, I am. Thank you.'

'Dare I ask why?'

'Well, all I can say is I had a wonderful night with Jenny last night.'

'I'm very happy for you, Robert. Don't forget our double date?'

'We are both looking forward to it, Sir.'

'Good, us too. Now Robert, we have work to do. Are you ready?'

'Yes Sir. Where do you want to start?'

'We have to interview Ventura again. He must tell us more about these killings. I'm hoping he'll also give up the other two names. My worry is the police physiologist will certainly declare him insane.'

'Do you think he's mad, Sir?'

'I'm not a doctor, Robert. But normal people don't do these kind of things.'

'I agree. But one of them was a doctor. That's unbelievable, don't you think?'

'Yes, I do. When I think of the times we stood in the mortuary listening to Doctor Cole giving his diagnosis and not knowing that he was one of the murderers'

'Makes me shudder just to think that I was in the same room as him. He seemed so normal, when all the time he was a sadistic killer.'

'Let's not dwell on it, Robert. Come on, we have work to do.'

In the custody suite, Sergeant Manning is on the phone. Police officers are running to the sound of an alarm coming from one of the cells. After what seems like hours Sergeant Manning puts down the phone and looks up at Shand and Walker waiting.

'I presume you want to speak to Mr Ventura?'

'If you can spare him for a while, Sergeant?'

'Very funny. Interview room number three is free. Sign here and he's all yours.'

The interview room is small furnished with one desk and four chairs. There are no windows. Harvey Ventura still handcuffed is shown to a chair, an officer goes to stand behind him. After the usual introductions Shand looks at Ventura.

'Mr Ventura, now you have had time to think and consult with your lawyer, are you prepared to cooperate with us?'

'That depends what you mean by cooperate, doesn't' it?'

'We have your signed statements for the four murders, plus the assaults on two police officers and the times and places they were committed. Even the way they were committed. You have been formally charged with these murders. I will ask you one last time Mr Ventura. Give me the names of the two other people who were with you?'

'Mickey fucking mouse, and Donald fucking duck.'

Ventura leans back in his chair grinning. Shand is shaking his head in disbelief.

'Very well, Mr Ventura, it seems you're not going to help us. I see no point in continuing with this interview.'

Shand leans forward to switch off the tape recorder. At the same time Ventura also leans forward and with a low and menacing voice whispers to Shand.

'Eat shit and die slowly copper.'

Back in his office, Shand is visibly shaken.

'I know it's early, Sir, but I've put a little 'extra' milk in your coffee.'

'Thanks Robert. What a repulsive person, this Ventura. I hope he spends the rest of his life behind bars.'

'I think that's a forgone conclusion, Sir. He's never going to walk the streets of this town or any other town again.'

'I just wish I knew who the other two people were. It's frightening to think they are out there somewhere.'

A copy of the Gazette lies open on the table showing the page of the resigning of the Bank manager and the Head master of the local school. Shand puts down his coffee mug covering the article. He returns to his desk, picks up one of the many files to be looked at. Walker puts his mug beside Shand's, turns to his computer and starts tapping away at the keyboard.

The trial only took two days. It was a closed court, as there were no witnesses to give evidence. Harvey Ventura was declared mentally insane and sent to an institution for the rest of his natural life.

The funerals of the victims were held in the local cemetery. The grief-stricken relations stood over the open graves sobbing, Shand and Walker felt they should be there as a mark of respect.

It was the end of the summer with a distinct chill in the air. Mrs Bruley and Mrs Jarvis where the only two mothers to attend the funeral of their sons. The other two victims Daniel Winter and Paul Fletcher were buried without ceremony in an unmarked grave.

Arthur Ambrose never regained consciousness and died in

his sleep. Doctor Cole was never found; a small boat was discovered abandoned off the coast of France. Frank de Caux and Clancy Belet both disappeared after resigning from their jobs, no one seemed to think there was anything suspicious in their sudden departure. They were both replaced within days of leaving.

Neal Shand went on holiday with Annabel Christi to Thailand where he proposed to her on a romantic beach at sunset. She accepted.

THE END

© Copyright R.J.Brophy 2014

CPSIA information can be obtained
at www.ICGtesting.com
Printed in the USA
BVHW041653290419
546847BV00016B/278/P